GETTING A LIFE

GETTING
A LIFE

Short Stories

by

Catherine Merriman

honno
MODERN FICTION

Published by Honno
'Ailsa Craig', Heol y Cawl, Dinas Powys,
South Glamorgan, Wales, CF6 4AH

British Library Cataloguing in Publication Data

A catalogue record for this book is available
from the British Library.

ISBN 1 870206 46 0

*Published with the financial support of
the Arts Council of Wales*

Cover illustration by Elizabeth Haines
Cover design by Olwen Fowler

Typeset and printed in Wales by Gwasg Dinefwr, Llandybïe

CONTENTS

ACKNOWLEDGEMENTS

Very many thanks to fellow Abergavenny writers Tricia, Mike T, Barbara, Mike M and Ewart, who were the first audience for nearly all these stories. Their advice and encouragement has been invaluable.

The following stories have been previously published or broadcast:

'Painting Juliet' in *Mr Roopratna's Chocolate* (Seren, 2000) and BBC Radio 4 (1999) (Abridged version).

'A Step Away From Trouble' in *Luminous and Forlorn* (Honno, 1994, ed. Elin ap Hywel).

'Aberrance in the Emotional Spectrum' in *Magpies* (Gomer, 2000, ed. Robert Nisbet).

'One Day' in *Mama's Baby, Papa's Maybe* (Parthian, 1999, ed. Lewis Davies and Arthur Smith).

'Delivery' in *Magpies* (Gomer, 2000, ed. Robert Nisbet).

'Primrose Hill' in *Planet* (1998) (longer version).

'Barbecue' in the *New Welsh Review* (1992), and *New Penguin Book of Welsh Short Stories* (1993, ed. Alun Richards).

MAMMARY ORGASMIC POTENTIAL
– A CASE STUDY

Georgina lost patience with the subject of Human Biology in 1967, when she was sixteen, after reading, in a much-hyped popular science book of the year, that fatty breast tissue in female humans had evolved in order to attract males. Till then, Biology had been her favourite GCE subject, her interest fostered by her ex-science teacher mother, who was a fan of Lorenz and Leakey and, since giving up her job on marriage, had become an ardent armchair ethologist. Young Georgina had limited experience of the world, and of men, but she was not lacking in common sense. The idea that in mankind's pre-monogamous past, males had played hard to get, or turned up their noses, so to speak, at flat-chested females, was preposterous. It was a fact, was it not (Georgina and her mother were anticipating Dawkins here) that the natural drive of every man was to attempt to plant his seed as often and as widely as possible, even if this ambition had been, in the more recent past, culturally curtailed. And the result of this would have been pregnancy – and so descendants – for all. If there ever had been intrinsically choosy or continent males, their lines would obviously and quite logically have died out. Indeed, it even occurred to Georgina

– though there was no mention of this idea in the literature, even to dismiss it – that men's bodies might have evolved to suit women; she knew that in the animal kingdom, at least, males were commonly excluded from the procreation business by a female penchant to welcome into their society and bodies only a limited number of strong and handsome males. Much less trouble all round, possibly. So the bodies of these males would have been shaped either by the females' needs and likings, or – and Georgina conceded that this might actually be more likely – by competition with their peers for access to the females. It was a red-letter day, brain-wise, the day she realized that the phrase 'dominant male' referred to dominance of a male over his fellow males, and only incidentally (in the sense that once a bully, always a bully) over females.

Of course, this was not to deny that males, in her society anyway, did find large breasts attractive. Or at least note-worthy. At street level, quite literally, Georgina (34DD) knew this, as suggested by unsolicited remarks such as 'wouldn't get many of them to the pound' or 'lor, luv, give us a handful', though the males offering such appreciation usually looked, in terms of present-day society, far from dominant. However, what males found attractive, indeed their general likes and dislikes regarding the female form, did not, Georgina felt, indeed could not, have influenced that form.

Georgina's irritation with evolutionary theory was, as it turned out, relatively short-lived (in the scale of things), because during the seventies – her twenties, which she spent in London working as a secretary – the world (or male biologists, rather) caught up with her, and belatedly acknowledged their mistakes. A new wave of evolutionary literature hit the bookstands, which put into words and so validated her private thoughts. One of these postulated a semi-aquatic past for early man, and suggested the development of floating, fatty breast tissue as an aid to breast feeding in water. This Georgina was happy to accept, partly because another breast-related question, only recently emerged, was now fascinating her. Okay, so breasts were fatty, floated, and under stimulation (such as sucking, as a baby might do) acquired teat-like nipples. Logical and sensible. But why were female human breasts so powerfully erogenous? For a while after this question occurred to her she imagined that it must have something to do with breast feeding – an inducement and reward for women suckling their young. The nipple was, undeniably, the focus of erotic sensation. But towards the end of the seventies, Georgina acquired both a husband, Hayden (one of those males grateful for fatty, floating, female breast tissue, but not tediously obsessed with it) and, a year later, a baby. Breast feeding, she discovered, was a pleasant activity, but hardly erotic. The sucking mouth of her son, while it certainly encouraged the teat-like shape of breast material, did not awaken the sensual threads that under her husband's stimulation, and indeed her own, could lead, with only a modicum of attention elsewhere, directly to orgasm. Under questioning, and in practical experimentation, Hayden denied that the same was true for him. Indeed, he found her experiments a mildly irritating (in both senses) waste of time. So why, Georgina wondered, did women have this facility; this double route to satisfaction, as it were, and not men? And, moreover, why were women capable of echo-orgasms (multiple orgasms, the magazines called them, having recently triumphantly discovered them) when men weren't?

She had plenty of time to ponder these questions because, as was normal for the times, she had given up paid work to care for her child. An interest in sexual biology and evolution had, she recognized, over the years, become her hobby. Her mother always said that everyone needed a private intellectual interest. A mental passion. She scoured the literature. Could it be that females needed more reward for intercourse, because the consequences of fertilization for their sex were profounder, and that to counter any caution this might engender they had therefore developed as more generally orgasmic? Or, to put it another way, women with low orgasmic potential avoided sex, because there wasn't a lot in it for them (grunting deadweights, complications of pregnancy, puerperal fever leading to certain death, etc) leaving their more enthusiastic sisters to provide the next generation? But did early humans understand the connection between sex and babies? If they didn't, well, even a low sex drive would probably result in almost perpetual pregnancy, and so gene-bearing descendants, and, if they did understand the connection, even so, wouldn't it, in those days, always have been a good idea, despite the risks, to have lots of babies? Wouldn't a big group of humans always have been more successful than a small group? And, if talking about a time so long ago that women had an oestrus cycle, a season, wouldn't they all have been at it with the enthusiasm of rabbits, hormonally driven, whatever the consequences? Oh, questions, questions. And what about the fact that women could enjoy sexual satisfaction very easily *without* the penetration required for conception and pregnancy? To where did that point? To a whole new direction?

It came to Georgina in the mid-eighties, at a time when her husband's sexual capacity seemed to be diminishing but hers was still increasing, that, despite the mysteries, there was one certainty about all this. This certainty was not an evolutionary explanation, but a simple, logical conclusion. Women, not men, were the true – if often latent

– sexual hedonists. Men could achieve orgasm only during the sex act, or in close simulation of it; women could have biologically satisfactory intercourse without orgasm (millions, apparently, did so regularly) but, crucially, were also capable of orgasm outside the sex act (or close simulation) without any penetrative element at all. Indeed, with only the slightest direct involvement of their lower, specifically reproductive organs. Women had achieved what men had not: the separation of the sex act from sexual pleasure.

There is something about discovering a facet of behaviour to be 'natural' that encourages acceptance of it. That reduces any guilt one might otherwise have felt regarding it. How many men, after reading Dawkins' *The Selfish Gene*, for instance, have not felt their wandering eyes excused? Sexual rampancy, they tell themselves, is part of their biological inheritance. Lust is all right. It's only natural.

So felt Georgina. Biology had not given her a body purpose-built for pleasure for nothing. It was there to be enjoyed. To explore its capacity was part of self-fulfilment. Almost a duty.

And she didn't have to behave destructively, or disloyally. Despite all her self-education, and the feminist times, she had no wish to break up her family. She liked Hayden. But, fortunately, nothing except her own body – well, breasts, to be specific – was required.

It was surprising how many normal, everyday activities orgasm could be incorporated into. And how little was required in the way of privacy. So much easier for women. Masturbating men seemed to need vigorous stimulation of the rudest area of their bodies – hardly an unnoticeable activity – plus the paraphanalia of visual triggers; women could achieve the same with much more discreet, oblique stimulation and had the invisible triggers of imagination and memory. Men discharged something at orgasm of a quantity that had to be dealt with. What women produced could safely be ignored. Just a matter of remembering to try it, really. Anything mentally (and preferably manually) untaxing would do. Showering. Exercise-biking. Sun-bathing. Watching television. Leaning against chest-high barriers . . . being put on hold when ringing public utilities . . . killing time in parked cars waiting to collect husband, son . . .

She was experimenting, of course. This was about pleasure, but not simple self-indulgence. She investigated how remote stimulation could be, breastwise, yet still trigger orgasm . . . the effects of different clothes and fabrics (and discovered the amazing efficacy of stiff taffeta over a peephole bra) . . . how many echoes could be achieved . . . how many repeats in 24 hours . . . she established the truth that the more you did it, the faster and better the result . . .

Eventually, innocently, she told Hayden – in broad terms – what she was doing. She hadn't planned to, and, if she had had time to think about it, possibly would have seen the dangers. But the subject of masturbation just came up, one evening, after they'd watched a Channel Four television programme about puberty. Hayden was reminiscing nostalgically about adolescence and the sadness of the single male. He seemed to be assuming that only teenagers and lonely men would indulge. She thought, well, I've got to tell him. He's obviously wrong. There was nothing to be ashamed of.

But Hayden was stunned. Didn't believe her at first – indeed, refused for a long time to accept that orgasm could be achieved exclusively via the breasts. It was idiotic – what, biologically, would be the point?

However, for a while – a couple of years, no less – the aftermath was gloriously positive. His sexual appetite increased dramatically, as if in appalled yet stimulated response. But then, in the early nineties, suddenly – almost overnight – waned to nonexistent. He had recently discovered that she was still masturbating. He seemed to give up. Retire defeated.

In 1995, when Georgina was forty-four, nine months after she and Hayden had last enjoyed successful penetrative sex, Hayden announced that he was having an affair with a work colleague. He said that while he was perfectly content to maintain their marriage at least until their son left home for college, he no longer wished to share a bedroom with her, or to be subject to any sexual contact. Georgina, who felt she had been a supportive, affectionate and sexually-compatible wife (and an easily good-enough mother) was distressed. She demanded to know why. 'Because I feel unneeded by you,' said Hayden. 'In fact quite redundant. And now I've found someone who does need me, and she's what I want.'

'For God's sake,' said Georgina. She translated the 'someone who needs me' to 'someone who needs me sexually' and thought this most unlikely. Unless the woman was ridiculously naive and inexperienced.

'I have never been unfaithful to you,' she complained. 'Never.'

Hayden set his jaw. Clearly he would have liked to dispute this but couldn't. 'The effect is the same,' he said mulishly. 'You have damaged my self-esteem. Unmanned me.'

Georgina refrained from saying, 'Well, balls-for-brain, that depends how you define yourself, doesn't it?' because she didn't honestly think that Hayden would have got as far as taking a lover if he wasn't serious, so there seemed little point. 'I don't see you as a pleasure machine,' she said. 'But as a loving friend who is the father of our child, and the man I have lived reasonably happily with for more than twenty years. My husband. However, if you feel as you do . . .'

'I do,' he said. 'I don't think you realise how important these things are to a man.'

Georgina didn't argue. Clearly he was right. Important to him, anyway. It was not until a few days later that it occurred to her that perhaps Hayden had been expecting her to forswear all masturbatory acts, now and forever, for the sake of his self-esteem and potency, and their marriage. Such a promise was obviously unthinkable; but it was sayable. No, she thought, stiffening her heart. Hayden was jealous of her sexual capacity. That was what it came down to. He wanted, and needed, to limit her potential, for his own selfish sake. As if he, and he alone, should control her pleasure. That was oppression, and she couldn't live with it.

Four years later, their son in his second year at Reading University, Georgina and Hayden divorced. The break up was as amicable as these things can be. They sold the family house and split the considerable proceeds. Hayden immediately moved in with his girlfriend, who had three small children from a previous marriage, and was certainly in a position to make him feel needed (domestically and economically, at least). Georgina spent a large sum of money visiting relatives in Australia and touring the Far East, and on her return decided to pursue her long-standing hobby in a more organised, academic fashion. Take up where she had lost patience, all those years ago. In the library opposite her sister's house (where she was temporarily staying) she scoured the further education prospectuses and discovered she could enrol as a mature student at the University of Greater Torrington for a degree in Human Biology that included the modules *Reproductive and Sexual Studies* and *Feminist Evolutionary Theory.*

She applied immediately and, in due course, was called for interview. During this she offered a short verbal presentation of her readings, thoughts and researches to date, and was offered an unconditional place on the spot. In her first semester the following September she found herself, unsurprisingly, streets ahead of all the other students.

She is now in her third year, predicted to get a First, and has already secured sought-after funding to stay on for an MA, the provisional title of which is *Mammary Orgasmic Potential – A Case Study.* The only downside of her new life is the procession of academics and fellow students – all male – who beat a path to her door, claiming to wish to assist in her research. She has told them to wait until she embarks on her PhD, where she hopes to pursue research that will challenge and open out the whole issue of human sexuality and function. The title, in her mind at least, will be *The Primitive and The Progressive: Gender Discrepancy in Sexual Evolutionary Development.*

EATING SUGAR

For a moment, emerging from the forest trail onto the deserted road, Alex thought they'd taken the wrong path down from the waterfall. A mad, dizzying thought. But, three hours ago, this forest clearing had been a busy market. He and his wife and daughter had stepped down from the open back of the Toyota songthaew after a hurtling five-mile ride from their beach bungalow into vivid colours and the scents of fish oil and lemongrass: a dozen or so food-stalls, half as many canvas-roofed bars. All vanished. Not even discarded litter to show for it. All that remained was a corrugated-iron toilet block, and the heavy trestles, benches and skeletal roof frameworks of the cafés. Plus the dark press of the rainforest around them.

'What's happened?' cried his wife Eileen. 'Christ! How do we get back?'

'It's all right,' Suzanne, their daughter, said soothingly. 'There'll be taxis along. Sit down and relax.' She swung her shoulder bag on to one of the hardwood trestle-tops and twisted her damp hair more securely in its scrunchie.

Alex sat down heavily on one of the benches. Even after the slow, downhill descent, undertaken immediately after prolonged immersion in the cool waters of the waterfall plunge pool, he was streaming with sweat. This awful,

16

drenching heat. As he tucked his foot under the bench his heel touched a giving object – the supine body of a sandy-coated hound-sized dog; it emerged, stretching, and scratched its ear with a back paw. They were astonishingly quiet and sweet natured, these ubiquitous yellow strays. Alex supposed they had to be, surviving on the random generosity of humans. Their first day in Thailand, thick-brained after the interminable flight, he had averted his eyes from the prostrate forms at the sides of the dusty roads. He'd assumed they were corpses. Traffic carnage. God knows, the Thais drove like men possessed. But then, strolling from the apartment complex in the evening, the temperature dipping to something approaching bearable, he'd been astonished to see two of the shapes rise, give stretching yawns, and pad purposefully towards the lights of a nearby restaurant.

The dog shifted to sit at Alex's feet and gazed up at him with soft yellow eyes. Alex's heart thudded in his chest.

'You OK, Dad?' Suzanne asked.

'Fine, fine. Just hot.'

'Why should a taxi come?' Eileen argued. 'It's not on the way to anywhere. The road stops here.'

'I'm sure she's right,' Alex murmured. 'It's a tourist attraction.'

Eileen found Thailand stressful, and wasn't ashamed to show it. Alex was grateful to her. Her constantly-expressed anxiety kept his own fear suppressed. Thailand in April. Idiocy. But forced on them; Suzanne was working out here as an English teacher, and the week of the Thai New Year holiday, Song Khran, was the only time she had off. A hundred degrees, even under lowering skies. Humidity that thickened the air, caused liquid to stream from the outside of anything cool. Every bar table awash. A debilitating, unhealthy, dangerous heat.

'Pass the water, Mum,' Suzanne said. Eileen dug in her bag – slow down, Alex urged her silently, don't scrabble, relax – and handed over the litre bottle.

'We weren't the last to leave the waterfall, were we?' he asked.

'There was a group of blokes,' said Suzanne. She swigged deeply from the bottle. You had to drink every half hour here. At least. An animal need that you were constantly aware of. 'Someone'll be along for them. It'll be OK.'

What was the alternative? They could walk back to the coast road. Three miles of narrow, pot-holed concrete through the forest. It would be dark in, what, an hour? Hour and a half? If they set off some time in the next half hour, they could do it. Maybe. They'd get appallingly overheated. Hideously insect-bitten. Christ. Maybe they couldn't.

But a taxi would come before then.

They should have joined the holidaying Thais leaving the waterfall. They'd set off an hour ago in beautifully behaved family groups, as if obeying a silent signal. Obviously they'd known the form, known when the day-time village and its transport departed. But it had been so tempting to have the place to themselves. All afternoon they had been the only westerners there. Farangs, as the Thais called them. White, high-status freaks. His daughter, at five ten, towered over most Thai men. He himself, at six two, was a giant. Women and children pointed and giggled behind tiny cupped hands.

Suzanne strode towards the corrugated-iron huts.

'Where're you going?' Eileen asked quickly.

'Where d'you think? Chill out, Mum.'

Alex nearly smiled. Chill out. Ha. Eileen panicked the moment Suzanne showed any inclination to stray. 'What if we got lost?' she'd asked daily in Bangkok. 'How would we find the flat again?' She was right, of course. He didn't want to think about it – their utter helplessness – but at least she did. In the suburb where Suzanne lived and worked they had seen no Farangs outside the apartment complex. Not one western face in the huge Carrefour supermarket down the thunderous dual carriageway. Eileen had been embarrassed at being the only woman there with bare shoulders. ('You should have told me, Suzanne.' 'Don't worry, Mum, they think we're all crazy anyway.') On the streets no one spoke English. Not even taxi drivers, policemen. Eileen carried the apartment address in her handbag, written in Thai script, which Suzanne had sent them in case of catastrophe at the airport, but most taxi drivers couldn't read even their own language.

It was the helplessness children must feel. There had been a role reversal here. Suzanne, their brave twenty-one-year old daughter transformed this side of the world to a competent, patient, encouraging parent. He and Eileen her anxious, fractious, dependent charges.

But there was no danger of getting lost here. Not now they were on Ko Chang. Ko Chang – Elephant Island – was one of the Thais own nature-reserve resorts. A single coast road with short inland spurs and minimal development – no structures higher than a palm tree, nothing inland from the beach strip at all. Directions to anywhere were simple. There might be other dangers, but not getting lost.

They heard male voices behind them. A sudden laugh, a crunching underfoot. Four stocky Thai men emerged from the narrow forest path. Alex swivelled on the bench and nodded a quick greeting at them. The man at the front, a dark-skinned muscular man maybe around thirty – difficult to tell the ages of Thais – grinned back at him. Then was distracted by his companions, who were waving their arms at the emptiness, uttering cries of astonishment. Clearly surprised also by the disappearance of the market.

Suzanne was striding back from the toilet block. The shed-like structure had its own spirit house on a pole alongside, Alex noticed. They looked like ornate hutted birdtables. This was jackdaw-decorated with glinting offerings. Well, yes. Heavens knows what malign spirits might otherwise lurk in a toilet block.

The mens' heads swung to his daughter as one. The man who'd just grinned at Alex flicked him another quick smile. He put his fingertips together and bowed a wai. Alex did the same.

'Engyish?' the man said. 'Eenglan?'

Too complicated to correct him to 'British'. And he'd never have heard of Wales. Alex nodded.

'Hay, hay,' the man crowed back at his friends. 'Ah.' He wai-ed respectfully at Eileen, then more deeply, theatrically, at Suzanne. 'Ah, fl'm staar.'

'No, actually.' Suzanne looked wearily amused, as if this was an unoriginal flattery. 'I'm a teacher.' She wai-ed and said something in Thai. Alex marvelled at her voice, the soft, lilting babytalk noise.

'Ahh!' cried the man. 'Not fl'm staar! Teasher! Speak Thai!' He swung round to his friends again, arms showman wide, then turned back and slapped at his chest, ecstatic, urging understanding.

'What's he trying to say?' asked Alex.

'Not sure. Oh, you too?' Suzanne's eyebrows shot high. 'You're a teacher too?'

The Thai nodded fervently. 'Oi, oi.' He waved at his friends and released a torrent of Thai. His companions laughed, nodded.

'Wirut,' the man said, banging his chest again. 'Wirut Srakan. Engyish teasher.' He pointed upwards and sideways, as if indicating somewhere over the tall forest trees. 'Eees, ees, long long way. Village. Big Surin.' He saw Suzanne's frown and tried again. 'Big *town* Surin?'

'Surin?' Suzanne's face cleared. 'Oh, yeah, right.' She turned to her parents. 'He's from the east, near Surin. And his name's Wirut. Wirut, that's right?' She checked with the Thai, who nodded eagerly. Speaking slowly she added, 'On holiday? Song Khran?'

'Holiday, yes, yes.' Wirut grinned widely. 'Ah speak Engyish, plees. Ah, Engyish, Engyish.' He sounded dreamy, like a man whose dearest wish has come true.

'Is he drunk?' Eileen hissed to Alex.

'He's from Eastern Thailand,' Suzanne said, hearing and reproving her mother. 'An Issan. Very rural. I don't suppose he meets many westerners. It's not like round Bangkok, or even up north. It's his subject, Mum. Imagine you taught, I don't know, Inuit in the depths of Snowdonia, and while you were holidaying on the Isle of Wight you suddenly bumped into an Eskimo.'

'Where's he staying? Ask him how's he getting back.' Eileen wasn't listening. Alex could tell from the glances she was giving Wirut's companions that she was wary of them. They were much less prepossessing than Wirut. One was heavily scarred facially, and the other two had missing teeth. It made their smiles unattractive. Alex was aware again of his heart thumping. There were four of them, and only himself, with his wife and daughter.

'We have to start walking soon,' muttered Eileen. 'You didn't bring the torch, did you?'

'No,' said Alex. 'Of course not.' The lack of street lighting on the island and regular power cuts meant a torch was a necessity. But it was on their mattress-side tiles in the primitive island bungalow, not here.

'I don't like this,' said Eileen. There was a tremor in her voice.

Anything could happen. That was what she meant. *Anything could happen.* And she was right. The first full day at Suzanne's flat, when they had gone to the supermarket to buy beers and breakfast food to stock their daughter's empty fridge, parked among the Toyota and Mercedes pick-ups in the car park had been an elephant. A stone's throw from the hurtling traffic of the freeway, a vast, loaded-up elephant. 'Elephant at supermarket,' Suzanne had piped in mock-pigeon English. 'Must be Thailand.' So many surprises. Nothing predictable. Nothing consistent. Modest Thai women covered their shoulders, swam – if at all, braving the water ghosts – in T-shirts and shorts, and didn't drink or smoke in public. While their sisters and brothers worked in a brazen sex industry, and small children sang along to pop songs about 'ladyboys'. Suzanne's elegant female boss advertised her school on the internet; but at weekends paid duty visits to the pampered cow that, in a previous existence, had been her alcoholic uncle. A mindset that was contradictory, incomprehensible. The Land of Smiles; but also of pirates, and bandits. A poor country where palaces were roofed in gold. 'Amazing Thailand', the billboards claimed; and, by God, they were right.

Eileen had started to walk restlessly around the clearing. Her eyes were fixed on the empty concrete of the road, snaking away into the greenery. Willing transport – taxi, songthaew, anything – to appear. She was twisting at the silver necklace she always wore.

Looking at her, Alex suddenly remembered an image from long ago, when Eileen had been their daughter's age. In the early seventies, restlessly pacing the small sitting room of their London flat. She had left the room abruptly, and, following her, he had found her in the kitchen shovelling spoonfuls of sugar straight from the bag into her mouth. She had taken a tab of LSD – as he himself had done – and was having a bad, deeply anxious, few minutes. There was a myth, in those days, that sugar was meant to bring you out.

There were parallels. The foreignness of Thailand was mind-expanding. You couldn't comprehend how different a culture could be till you experienced it. A perceptual door was opened that could never be reclosed. And there was a surreal quality to the experience, your senses, understandings, constantly challenged. But after the sugar moment Eileen had gone on to enjoy herself; no, more than that – to marvel at the sensory richness of a normally invisible, unguessed-at world. She had never regretted that single experimental trip.

Something was biting the back of his calf. He slapped at himself.

'Want the Jungle Juice?' Suzanne said. 'It's in Mum's bag.'

'Ah,' said Wirut, noticing. 'Bare bare. Bare good.'

'Sorry?' said Alex.

'Bare?' Wirut looked quizzically at Suzanne. Mimed glugging from a bottle.

'Beer,' said Suzanne.

'Beer, yes yes, beer.'

'He's suggesting beer as an insect repellent. Taken internally.'

Wirut got one of his companions to unload the small pack from his back. He pulled out a brown bottle. And two more. 'Beer, yes? You join us. Beer. Engyish, Thai, teeshers, frens.'

'I don't think he speaks terribly good English for an English teacher,' Eileen said tartly, returning from her stroll. She looked much more in control now. Gathered together.

'Here, sit please.' Wirut waved them over, indicating they share the trestle table with his companions.

Alex hesitated.

'Accept,' Suzanne urged. 'It's rude not to. And he'll love it. He's an Issan. Yokel Thai. Farangs at his table.'

Alex said, 'Thank you,' with a small nod of his head. He rose and joined the Thais. The yellow dog followed and reseated itself a yard away. Wirut opened one of the beers and plonked it on the wood in front of him.

'Dring, dring,' he urged.

Alex drank deeply. *Chang* beer. Cool, tasty beer. Up at the waterfall they must have stored it in the chilled water. Christ, it was good. Wirut was waving another bottle at Eileen.

'Go on, Mum,' said Suzanne. 'I'm going to have one. Thank you, Wirut,' she said, articulating clearly. 'We are very happy, very grateful.'

Wirut looked delighted. He swigged from his own bottle, his eyes crinkling with good humour. But Thais smile all the time, Alex thought. Even when they don't like you at all.

'How are you getting home?' Suzanne asked Wirut. 'Songthaew? Taxi?'

'Yes, yes.' Wirut waved a careless hand at the road. 'Yes. Car come soon.'

'Does he mean one's definitely coming, or he expects one will come?' Eileen picked up the beer bottle Wirut had opened for her, and sat down beside Suzanne. The other men were the far end of the trestle, talking noisily in Thai.

'I don't know,' shrugged Suzanne.

Eileen tipped the bottle to her lips and drank deeply. She wiped her mouth with the tips of her fingers. 'And he said car. We can't all fit in a car.'

Alex heard the words, and looked up. She should have sounded anxious. But she didn't. So no one was responding, reassuring her. Reassuring him. He felt suddenly deserted. Eileen was taking another swig from her beer bottle, lowering it with a sigh of satisfaction. Suzanne was digging in her shoulder bag, extracting – what? – her diary notebook. Both lulled, seduced, into acceptance.

He was responsible for them.

And he, alone, could see the peril they were in.

A suffocating balloon rose in his chest. He pushed the beer away abruptly and struggled out of the bench seat. The yellow dog backed away from him.

'I think we have to go,' he said. 'I don't think we can risk waiting here. It's going to be dark very soon.'

'Don't be silly, Dad,' scoffed Suzanne. 'Sit down.'

'No,' said Alex. How dare she speak to him like that? In front of strangers. Had she been right about taxis appearing? No, she hadn't. And she'd always been far too trusting. Always. Often in trouble because of it. You didn't become a different person just because you were the other side of the world.

'I think it would be sensible to make a start,' he said. Not that he felt remotely sensible. The sense of fear, now it was cracked open, was awful. He needed to break away, move, start walking. Would the Thais let him? Wirut's face was averted and neutral, as if he hadn't noticed what was happening. Patently a pretence, a sham. Oh Christ.

He strode away from the bench. The others would follow. They'd have to. This place was dangerous. Danger on all sides. The heat. The dark. The men. The forest. God, the forest. The voracious tumultuous forest. You were so aware, here, of civilisation as ephemera. How, if you just turned your back, all would revert to wilderness. Empty lots in the middle of Bangkok sprouted, almost overnight, lush vine-hung vegetation. There were snapping fish the size of small sharks in the canals, the klongs. Tales, even, of crocodiles. Every house had its ceiling geckoes and wall-crack lines of Pharaoh ants. The wooden bar table that he just risen from, left unused for a couple of weeks, would probably shoot new, rampant growth.

Eileen called from behind him. 'Alex! Wait!' He stopped,

but didn't turn. Footsteps strode up behind him. Not Eileen, though. Suzanne.

'Don't freak out, Dad,' she said kindly. 'It's really uncool in Thailand.'

'For God's sake,' snapped Alex. 'Listen to yourself. We've got to do something.'

'No. We haven't.' Suzanne smiled at him as if he was an overwrought child. 'We're fine.'

'Those men.' He flicked his eyes back. Eileen was actually chatting to Wirut now. 'Suppose they're, well, Christ, they could be up to anything . . .'

'They offered you a beer, Dad. Why'd they do that if they were up to something?'

'I don't know. But it proves nothing. And it's getting dark. By the minute. What'll happen if we get stuck out here all night?'

'We won't. Even if we did, nothing terrible would happen. We've got toilets, piped water. It's not as if there are tigers out here. But you heard Wirut, he says a car'll come. Even if there's no room for us, he'll send a taxi when they get back to the coast road. They're nice people, Dad. I'm sure.'

Alex closed his eyes. I know I'm right, he thought despairingly, because the situation is so obviously dangerous. And I've seen deceit in Wirut's face. I want – need – to protect my wife and daughter. But I am so hot I can't make a fight of it. I haven't the energy. I just want this over. To be out of here.

'Dad,' said Suzanne. She laid a hand on his arm and tugged at him. He felt himself move. She was pulling him back towards the bench. 'Wirut's got some of those fruits you like. The ones that taste of lychees? Sit down and have a beer. Everything's going to be alright.'

She was speaking to him as if he was ill. Perhaps he was. A heat-induced fever. But thinking this didn't help. The terror was still inside him, flapping its awful wings.

As they drew close to the Thais Alex tried to collect himself. Wirut glanced his way. His eyes were dark, evasive. But then he grinned, suddenly pantomime host again, and waved a bottle at him. 'Ah, sit, sit.'

Alex sat down at the bench and drained half the contents of the new bottle in one gulp. Recklessly, irresponsibly. He had tried to warn the others, and they didn't believe him. What more could he do?

Wirut placed fruits like small soft-spined chestnuts in a line on the table before him. 'Eat,' he urged.

OK, thought Alex, I can do that. I can eat. Play games with you. He picked up one of the fruits and dug his nails into the flesh. Ridiculous, sea-urchin-like fruits. Almost cute. They stuck together like teasel heads. The white insides were delicious, though: a sweet, elderflowery pulp.

He looked at the row on the tabletop. He's feeding me, he thought. Trying to take my mind off what is happening. Trying to distract me from the darkening forest where I sit with my family, miles from anywhere, with no safe future ahead of us, in the company of four unknown Thai men.

Suzanne was writing something in pencil at the back of her diary notebook. Her address, apparently, to be swapped with Wirut's. Eileen got up from the table murmuring that she'd just use the loos, before it got too dark to find them.

Alex let the activities of others pass over him. His jaw muscles were so tense he could hardly chew. Whatever was going to happen would happen soon. It would be quite dark in fifteen minutes. These terrible moments had to pass.

He took another swig of beer from the bottle and found, as he lowered the bottle to the wooden table top, his eyes resting on the yellow dog, which was still sitting beside them. Still quiet, patient, unassertive. He gazed into the animal's calm, fatalistic eyes. This dog would remain here all night. The daytime market would be its territory. It wasn't asking to be taken away, rescued from this place. It wasn't afraid of the forest. Or the men. Thais were Buddhists, they killed no animals, except for food. Not even flies.

There was a rumbling in the air. Alex looked skywards. Thunder? The heavens grumbled regularly here. No. An engine? Wheels on concrete? His eyes strained into the gloom.

'Car come?' said Wirut, cupping a hand ostentatiously to his ear.

There were lights in the distance, headlights, definitely.

A car was coming. Crunch time. Whatever was going to happen, would now happen. Either the Thais would go, and he and his family would be left here alone, or . . . Alex could feel the panic rising again, like vomit in his throat.

The vehicle was black, huge, storming through a dust cloud towards them. A Mercedes. A Mercedes pick-up. He swallowed the panic. Oh God, a flash of hope. A pick-up.

Wirut was grinning triumphantly at him, his eyes urging relief. Alex held his gaze, and saw the man. No pretence. The real man. He felt his fear drain away. A physical sensation, like being doused with cool water. How stupid he'd been. Of course Wirut had been acting earlier, feigning blindness. What else could a good-hearted, tactful Thai do, faced with a panicking Farang? Losing your cool was almost a crime in Thailand.

Wirut strode proudly towards his car. His monster, Farang-rescuing car. 'You ride back or cab?' he threw over his shoulder. 'Hey yeh!' he shouted, as the vehicle crunched to a vibrating halt. The smiling young man driving the beast slapped his hand against the outside panel of the door.

'Here's our lift, Dad,' Suzanne murmured in Alex's ear.

Eileen hurried across from the toilet block. 'Oh wow,' she gasped. 'I want to ride in the back.'

Two of Wirut's friends climbed into the cab with the driver. The other leapt up the dropped tailgate and beckoned at them.

Wirut helped Eileen into the back of the pick-up. His friend smacked the rubber of a spare tyre lying flat, encouraging her to sit on it. Suzanne jumped up and sat beside her. Alex accepted a heave-up – his muscles were actually weak with relief – and sat on the floor opposite. The pick-up was huge. He stretched an arm up to the roll bar.

Wirut handed out bottles of beer. 'Careful teeth,' he snorted, miming being jolted over a bump. He stood over them and slapped his palm on the top of the cab. The engine revved, and they were roaring off down the concrete.

'God!' screeched Eileen, snatching at the bar. They were suddenly battered with hot wind. The dark forest, high on either side, had become a solid, roofless tunnel. She tossed her hair and laughed in delight. 'This is the way to travel!'

The rushing air was wonderful against the dampness of Alex's skin. Energy, life, was flooding back into him. For a blissful minute he simply savoured it. Then gave a smiling nod at Wirut and raised his voice. 'All the way from Surin?' He patted the floor of the pick-up.

'Eh?' Wirut bent over him smiling, eager to understand.

'Your car!' shouted Suzanne. 'From Surin?'

'Ah, yes, yes! Good car, yes?'

'*Very* good,' said Alex.

The car slowed marginally, then swung sharply right.

'The coast road,' said Suzanne. 'That didn't take long.'

'We sing, yes?' Wirut announced. 'Pop songs, Engleesh, yes?'

'Your department, I think,' Alex said to Suzanne. He glanced sideways. 'Oh wow . . .'

An illuminated forest had appeared, between the coast

road and the sea. Huge beach palm trees with gracefully curved trunks, festooned, right to their arching, feathery tops, with white fairy lights. The sea, the backcloth between the trunks, was black velvet, edged with frothy strips of brilliant white foam. Like an elaborately decorated stage set. How incredibly Thai. Alex felt he had never seen anything so beautiful.

Eileen started to sing, *'I've been a wild rover for many a year . . .'*

Alex laughed, his eyes still on the magical lights. Another reminder of their youth – his and Eileen's youth. When they had hitched to Yugoslavia, earned dinars busking on the streets of Dubrovnik. Long-haired innocents, up for anything.

They'd been brave too, in those days. And experimental And, yes, indeed – how could you not be? – trusting.

He joined in the chorus with gusto.

PAINTING JULIET

'What is it about plants?' Juliet asked, after the dozenth time I refused to paint her portrait.

I plucked a herbaceous attribute from the air. 'The stillness,' I said.

A good one. She didn't know whether to freeze, vegetable-like, or rant, her-like.

She wants me to paint her portrait. I'm not that kind of artist, I say. Not any more. I'm capable of it, of course, but I never paint girlfriends. Even frisky, amusing, twenty-eight-year-old girlfriends, who take inexplicable shines to middle-aged daubers. Call it tact, if you like. Or cowardice. I draw plants, not portraits. A portrait is a front(ish) view of a human being. Artists, despite our fleeting pretensions, are mere humans too, and human beings interact. Juliet and I have been interacting for several months. If I paint her portrait, I won't be painting an object, which just happens to be a person. I'll be painting a relationship.

Not a problem with plants. Interaction is not one of their strengths. Obligingly passive, undemanding things. Perfect sitters. They don't give a toss what they look like, leaves all askew, the odd petal droop – a matter of total indifference. They're happy to hold a pose for hours, or not hold it; they don't get miffed if you decide to take photos and work from them instead. You don't have to talk to them; though you can, of course, and their discretion is absolute. Nor do they object if you have a fag or a drink without offering them one, or fart or belch in their presence.

And, you know, there's a lot more demand for pictures of plants than of people. Oh yes. Take a look in your bookshelves. How many gardening books have you got? Plant identification books? Nature books? Use a lot of sketches, paintings, don't they? Now, how many books of human portraits have you got? None? Thought so. We all have a living to make.

I am sketching a nice docile yucca at the moment. Four feet high, with the appearance – and I know I'm hurting no one by saying this – of an upturned floor mop. *Yucca elephantipes.* So named, I assume, because the woody trunk suggests the emaciated leg of a midget elephant. She – all plants are female, obviously – is not a perfect specimen (two tatty fronds, as if a cat's taken passing exception to her) but I am drawing her as if she were. Now, could I do this with Juliet? No. Juliet is Juliet. It is precisely Juliet's unique peculiarities that make her Juliet. The yucca-ness of my friend here, on the other hand, is independent of such things. Her individual characteristics are irrelevant.

OK, I anticipate Juliet's objection. I'm not comparing like with like. The equivalent to 'yucca', as a generic, I suppose, should be 'human'. But try drawing a human, in the same detail I draw my yuccas. Does it end up simply 'human'? Does it hell. It ends up old, young, male, female, fat, slim, fair, dark. A unique, if sketchy, individual. There is no such thing, pictorially, as simply 'human'. Moreover, this individual, drawn with only cursory detail, wears an expression. Happy, sad, angry, contrite, bored, excited. Decisions, decisions. You wonder why I prefer drawing plants?

Juliet's women friends assume I must have painted or

drawn her. He's an artist, is he? they say – giving me, if I'm present, a look half appraising (so *that's* an artist) half, well, *arch*, as if at any moment I might do something rampantly unconventional, possibly of a sexual nature. 'So,' they murmur, 'where are the pictures of you?' 'Nowhere,' Juliet replies, stiffly. The stiffness suggests that the admission, in a small way, humiliates her. Thus it is, undoubtedly, a criticism of me.

Would a plumber plumb the home of his girlfriend? A mechanic service her car? An architect design her house? Hell – I'm exampling myself into a corner; the answer's probably yes. Ah, but no. The trades are different, aren't they? How many ways are there of fixing a tap washer? Afterwards, the tap either drips, or it doesn't. Same with an engine – it runs sweet, or it doesn't. And the design of a house; well, no one would design a house for a girlfriend without consulting her, finding out what she wants. It would be a shared project; his execution moulded by her needs and desires.

While a portrait. It would be *for* her, but with no input *from* her, except as subject matter. Portraits express the artist's view of the subject, not the subject's view of themselves. And here, we're getting to the crunch. She wants my view of her. I don't want to give it to her.

Well, got there in the end. Forget all the tosh. We're good at making everything their fault, aren't we? The fact is that if I paint her portrait – a proper portrait, not a camera-snap equivalent – I will be revealing myself to her – myself, vis-à-vis her – and this I balk at.

I have told her. An attempt at honesty. The reason I won't paint your portrait, I say, is because, if I do it properly, I would be exposing myself to you (don't snigger) with no reciprocation. And, I add (on thinner ice now, but mere exposure doesn't seem enough), what I revealed would, in all probability, be scoffed at by you. I'd be making myself vulnerable. The old boy-girl thing. Loin-girding approach by boy, castrating rejection by girl.

'For God's sake,' she says, rolling her eyes. 'Don't be ridiculous.'

'No,' I say firmly. 'It's you who's ridiculous. There is no guarantee you'd like it. It might even offend you.'

This is a mistake. The thin ice shatters. 'Since when,' she hisses, 'did offending me worry you? And when have I ever, *ever* scorned your work?' She exits violently, frightening the door. It shakes for several seconds. But she returns later, much calmer. 'What I'd really appreciate,' she says, in a quiet, reasonable voice, 'is the mere fact that you'd painted my portrait. That's more important to me than what the picture looks like.'

'Good heavens,' I say. 'Really? So you wouldn't need to see it? I could just slap the paint around, prove I've done it, and then hide it away somewhere?'

She smiles tolerantly. What a joker. Explains that of course she'd want to see it. She's just promising that she'll be nice about it. Take into account its existence, the work that went into it, as well as its actual appearance.

Terrific. So now she's saying that she will want to see the picture, and will absorb any information it conveys (because how can she not?) but will keep her response to this, tactfully, to herself. What an offer. Not only will she be privy to my true, artistically expressed feelings about her, but her reaction to these feelings will remain under wraps. How can I refuse?

'Anyway,' she cajoles, 'what will be so revealing about the portrait? What have you got to hide?'

This is a very intelligent question. Juliet – contrary to any impression I might have given – is very intelligent. Another way in which she differs from plants. The answer, of course, is that I don't know – I can't know – until I paint the portrait. Like any act of creation, it is a process with an unknown end. Not totally unknown – it will, at least in my own mind, centre on Juliet, or some vital aspect of her – or, indeed, us – but how, exactly, remains to be seen. After all, if you knew what the end-product of a creative work was going to be, why bother with the toil of getting there?

This interests her. (I have foolishly argued my case aloud.) A voyage of discovery. 'Yeah,' I say. 'Me voyaging, you discovering.'

'You discovering too,' she cries, 'and so what?' She is pink with frustration. (Quite an interesting pink, traces of carmine.) 'It's not a contest,' she says. 'Who can hide most from whom. We're meant to be in love.'

This is true. We are. Meant to be. OK, I say. I have a problem. I admit it freely. Us problematic males do. You females can lay your hopes and fears and needs and desires on the slab for anyone to pick over, but we blokes value our privacy. We are mysterious creatures, even to ourselves, and that's how we like it.

'Aha!' she cries. 'Aha! So it's not *my* reaction to a portrait that's stopping you, it's *yours*.'

For a moment I am dumbfounded. 'I didn't say that,' I mutter.

'Yes, you did,' she retorts.

See, you don't get this with yuccas. They don't tire your brain. Answer back. Provoke you into saying things that may or may not be true.

OK, I say finally, because I refuse to be drawn into further argument. God knows where it'll end. Capitulate now. You win. I'll do it. She claps her hands. I have delighted her, and that's a nice feeling. Extraordinarily nice. I hadn't anticipated that. But there are rules, I say sternly. She nods. Anything, anything. Anything, eh? Wickedness tempts, but a carte blanche forces responsibility. Why am I so mature, dammit? So here they are: all reasonable rules. First, no looking till it's finished. Nod nod nod. She expected that. Understands I can't work with eyes over my shoulder. Especially not hers. Second: no enquiries over progress. No 'how's it going?' even. Nod nod nod. Oh those bright, forget-me-not eyes. Third and last – no demands for explanation when it's over. The picture must be enough. I'm a visual artist. If I wanted to explain myself verbally, I'd be something else.

We are agreed. We have set aside time. I'm nervous, but it's a stewing nervousness, not unpleasant. It promises a result. First, the sketches. This is the part I particularly don't want her to see, or comment on, because it can stop me dead. I'm good at sketching. It's what I do, if I'm honest, when I draw my plants. It's all they want. A clear, painted-in sketch. She'd like these sketches of mine. If I painted one in, that would probably be enough. For her, that is. But if I'm going to do this at all, let's do it properly. Let's do it for me. Sketches are just the starting point.

It's the hand moving that stimulates the brain. When the hand is free, experimental, unrestrained. No way of knowing which way to go until I've roughed it out, seen it. Recognised it. Takes a lot of sketches, but she's being patient. And, I have to admit, she's a lovely subject to draw. My hand feels comfortable. Doesn't dither. Seems to know intuitively where to go.

Right. I've decided on a whole body portrait. I've tried heads, and head and shoulders, but they all look decapitated. Partial. I need the whole of her. And I don't want background detail. Nothing that suggests a setting. Juliet does not belong anywhere. She is just Juliet. So. Standing? Sitting? Lying? Naked? Clothed?

She has a green dress I keep getting flashes of. A soft sheath dress, clingy T-shirt material. I've asked her to put it on, and it looks kind of right. But only kind of. Nakedness appeals too, though not for the obvious reasons. Not even because it suggests intimacy. And not even because I can see she likes the idea. Wanton woman – the point of this is to satisfy me, not indulge her. But she does look good naked. Confident, natural.

I'll start with nakedness; see how it runs. I can always overpaint. I need her standing, legs together. Weight on one hip if she wants to. As long as she's upright, and doesn't give me daylight between her thighs. She's tall and slim. Lying or sitting you wouldn't see it, and tall and slim is her. Her for me, that is.

Well, I've got a general painty outline, and even the brush strokes to go with it, but her middle section is proving a problem. Her breasts, particularly. Not sure why, but they are. Bloody things. Too substantial. Too fleshy. Too animal. I need lightness, less solidity.

But I'm going to enjoy the hair. Wild red hair. Pile on the henna, I've told her.

Shit. Something isn't working. Stand back. It's not right. Juliet can see my face.

'Problems?' she says, deeply sympathetic. She's been a dream since I started doing this; no criticism, nothing's too much trouble. A revelation.

'Shut up,' I reply. 'I'm thinking.'

She's not offended. Not remotely. She's flattered. All this wrestling concentration, over her. Except it isn't, of course. It's over me.

It's no good. Start again. I repaint the canvas. Green. The entire thing. A plain green canvas. And for a terrible few hours that's where I want to leave it. As if the colour says it all. She would be appalled, but that's not my consideration. I am appalled at myself. It shows a lack of complexity. A mental laziness, even.

Face it, I am a lazy bugger. It's years since I've done this. Years of sketching plants, painting them in, no effort at all. Story of my life. Yes, the story of my life.

Dim, too. I say it to myself, hear it in my ears, and still take hours to grasp it. The green is right. But as background. It's where she comes from.

Yes! Got it. Got it. Christ, I even understand it. No, wait, it rings bells. It's been done before. Hell. But does that matter? Think, think. No. It's OK. The reference works. The image is right. If I can capture it.

Juliet is delighted with my attitude. My commitment. This is a side of me, she says, she has been longing to see. A true artist. When not fighting with the painting I am distracted and monosyllabic; I can't think what she finds attractive about this, but there's no accounting for female taste. I am slightly proud of myself, though. I do feel committed. And, dammit, I am enjoying myself. Who'd have thought it?

I've put as much green as I can get away with into her skin tone. She's got to be distinct from the background, but connected to it. As if she has *emerged* from it. I think it works. I've solved the breast problem. I was getting hung up on what they actually looked like, rather than what I felt about them, and her. A change of perspective, that's all it took. Now there they are: as fragile, blow-in-the-breeze as the rest of her. Not that I see women's flesh as fragile, you understand – anything but – but fragile it has to be. Fragility suggests all the right things: preciousness, perfection, the sense of something caught between too-soon (sturdily immature) and too-late (wilted, overblown). It means extraordinary, undeserved luck.

Good God. Listen to me. Sentimental fool.

Now I'm buzzing. This is right right right. All those years of practice, and I'm within tendrils of the end. I am reassured, pathetically, by the fact that Juliet will never know my journey here. Silly me; of course I'm safe. She thinks I've been at the point I've just discovered for months, and she'll never know otherwise.

She was absolutely right, too, about the act of painting being more important than the final appearance, though not in the way she meant. She was thinking about herself, not me.

There we are. Complete. Perfect. The image, necessarily, is more abstract than Juliet might have wished, but it's right, and that's what matters. She'll recognise herself. I haven't played around with her face; it's unmistakeably her. Doing that didn't even feel like a concession. In fact it felt essential. Ambiguity about her identity would be a cop-out.

Stand back from it. Look at those hands. An Amaranthus would be jealous. And the burnished hair – eat your heart out, Acer Purpurea. Glad I chose lily rather than orchid between her legs. Orchid's more genital but too obvious, and lily's more approachable, and just as sexy. My Woman of Flowers. The original, if you remember your folk tales, was a lady specially created to partner some poor sod cursed never to have a mortal wife. She was unfaithful to him and in the end conspired to kill him. Well, yes. Women aren't floral Lego. Take one on, and they can hurt you.

Wonder if Juliet knows the story? Maybe, maybe not. I'll show it to her now. But no explanations. I warned her.

BEYOND WORDS

Outside the bathroom window, out in the brave new gusty (gutsy?) world, clouds sang, and birds scudded across the blue. The bath water she had just stepped out of swirled, gurgling, all the way down to Australia. Soft white towelling-turf pampered her body dry.

A creative day. No doubt about *that*. And creation required sustenance. So, for breakfast, she had a fetal chicken. No she didn't. Only positive thoughts allowed. It would never have been a chicken. Simply fetal-chicken food. Ugh, horrid. Call it egg.

Then a quick check on Giles – asleep, as he always was after the visiting nurse's ministrations, poor lamb – and out across the lush plain of the June lawn, to the summer house. (Gazebo? Pavilion?) She opened the door and stood motionless, trying to identify the components of the olfactory invasion of her nostrils. A writer's duty, to *name*. Heady, resinous wood odour. Confined, overripe heat. Hot glass. Giles used to say you couldn't smell glass, but, when it was hot, of course, of course, you could.

Oh bugger. Some small mammal was living in here – there was black vermicelli scattered across the golden boards under the window. Very likely a field mouse. Oh well – what was that to an artist? In tune with the natural world. She made a humming noise at the back of her throat. Literally in tune. God, what a spiritual sound.

She seated herself in the wicker chair in front of the fold-away table and opened her laptop. Good thing she didn't use paper and pencil. They'd probably be the raw material for a nest by now.

Actually, that was a rather attractive idea. A resonant idea. Words as nest. Words as succour, protection. Yes. Maybe she could develop that . . .

She opened the file she'd been working on the last time the creative urge had come upon her. God. More than a fortnight ago. Well, yes, of course it would be. Giles' crisis, last week. Every waking hour occupied, physically or mentally. Don't think about it. How illness swallowed time.

And what was this, less than a page? In half a day? Well. Assembling words devoured time, too.

> *Desire.*
> *Inexpressible. Words catch not even the corner of it, shoot past even approximation, hit a target that is either trite and laughable, or anatomical and pornographic. Like a tidal wave on the horizon, looming, threatening, enthralling, a wave that never reaches wordland, except as spin-off slops of froth, or the crash of a few brutal breakers, or the lap lap of insipid nothingness . . .*

She scrolled down to the last sentence.

> *Oh, three cheers for desire, for escaping the constraints of words, for reminding us that there is life beyond language.*

Humph, she thought, frowning over the screen. Where had that come from? She tried to remember back. It had been hot. Yes. She had had the doors open. Sunshine on her bare arms. Exquisitely sensual, the warmth of the sun. Oh dear. The ring of a cri-de-coeur, dressed up as something more, something objective, exploratory. And it wasn't going any-where, was it? In fact it seemed to have written itself into a blank page.

She sighed deeply, and opened a New Document. Forget about desire. Yesterday's topic; well, a fortnight-ago's topic. Today, a new inspiration. Words. Nest. Succour.

She hesitated, thinking. Her gaze rested on the mouse droppings. Mice. Sharing her creative space with mice. Mice didn't need words. Their entire life was wordless. They were born, grew up, foraged for food, copulated, constructed nests, had babies, brought them up, died, peacefully or violently, all without words.

Lucky, lucky mice. No handed-down history. No accumulated knowledge. No fear, except of the immediate. If, for instance, a mouse were to develop a small limp, a minor weakness of the leg, for example, for no apparent reason, that would be all it was – a small limp. A minor weakness. The mouse wouldn't worry about it; it would either manage, or it wouldn't. No other knowledgeable expert mouse would explain what it could be, what it might be, what, as the dysfunction worsened, spread, it unfortunately, certainly, was. The lack of words kept mice safe from contemplations of their future.

She had drifted entirely off the point.

Words as nest. Words as protection. Words as succour. Ease. Comfort.

Or had she? Perhaps there was a paradox here? Perhaps she could tease one out. Wordless animals, in a nest of presaging words . . .

Oh, God. She sighed again. Why was she starting here? Texture, texture. Always the seduction of texture. Beautiful, pointless words, metaphors, paradoxes. Where was the *story*? That was what was needed. Where was the narrative, the movement, the thing that was happening, to hang the word-texture on.

Trouble was, she didn't think in terms of things happening. How could she? In this beautiful, constant, unhappening garden. Professionally tended, perpetually perfect. All the bedding plants in last week. The tubs filled. Scented plants, she had asked for. Plants that would perfume the air outside Giles' wide-flung windows.

Words as refuge. Words as escape.

Oh, why couldn't she be a potter? Or a watercolourist? Even a gardener.

And yet, she was lucky. Of course she was. She was an artist. She assembled words, an activity which gave her huge pleasure. She had no material wants – oh, thank Giles eternally for his foresight, his prudence, his insurance policies. How many husbands provided so generously for their wives? Even when that husband couldn't, literally, lift a finger for himself. To be able to stay in this large secluded house with its paradise garden. A nurse twice daily, morning and evening, to help her keep him alive, and as comfortable as possible.

And she had time. Time and time and time.

Words as consolation. Words as substitute.

And, quite soon, something would happen. Giles's elbow-buzzer would go, or ominously wouldn't, and something would have happened. Very soon, in fact, the expert mouse had said.

How could she pre-empt that?

A STEP AWAY FROM TROUBLE

On my way up to Clive's in Brynmawr I stop off at the Corn Exchange pub in Gilwern. I've got a spare helmet on the back of the XS because I half expect Bethan to need a lift, but she isn't here; her brother Kev must have taken her in the van.

I try not to notice Doggy, hunched over a glass the far end of the bar. It's only nine-thirty and he looks stewed already. He walked out on his wife Rose three months ago but the bachelor life don't seem to be bringing him joy.

As I order my pint I'm aware he's sidling up to me. He's on the whisky and his eyes are mean. He stares at me.

'Surprised you aren't screwing Rose too,' he says nastily.

I reckon I've come in at the tail end of a conversation he's having with the whisky.

'Ta,' I say with a polite smile. 'But I prefer to roll my own.'

Doggy scowls; he wants to have it both ways and feel insulted that I haven't screwed his wife, but isn't quite smashed enough. He soon will be though, and I'm out tonight to enjoy myself, so I down my pint fast.

The encounter's still niggling me as I pull out on to the Heads of the Valley's road, and instead of going straight to Brynmawr I decide to cut up through Llanelly Hill and take a detour to Blaenavon. Drop in on Rose. No carnal

motives, mind – just to spite Doggy and say howdo to a
mate. Why shouldn't she have callers? Miserable bastard,
Doggy is.

It's a clear dry night – asking for the scenic route. I
power up through the beechwoods to the Hill and take a
left on to the Blaenavon road. Over a thousand foot up
here, and it's a lost world – grassed over spoil tips and
hummocky workings, derelict sheds, lonely strips of run-
down terraces. At night the bike lights funnel you through
the blackness. I take the Whistle Inn straight so fast the
cattle grid's just a sizzle in my spine.

Then I'm at the Big Pit tourist signs and slowing down
for Blaenavon. I cut into the back streets across the main
road – Rose's flat is on the eastern slopes, half a hillside
above the centre of town. I trundle the bike through the
steep narrow roads, past a line of lock-ups, and prop it by
the main entrance of the flats. Hers is on the first floor
in the front. It seems to be in darkness but I ring the bell
anyway.

She's in; I see a moon face checking at the window, and
then the door buzzes open. Bike boots make a helluva
clomp up concrete stairs. Rose's on the landing outside her
door in bare feet, cycling shorts and a baggy T-shirt. Had a
laid-back day, lucky girl.

'Hiya,' she says, waving me into the flat. None of the
lights are on but I can hear the telly in the sitting room. She
says she's conserving power because she's only got one
token left for the meter, and she must catch *Cell Block H* at
midnight.

It takes me a moment in the gloom to see she's got
company. On the leatherette settee there's a pair of gleaming
white thighs, shifting position.

'This is Tanya,' Rose says. 'From up the road.'

'Hi,' I say. I've found a face, round and puddingy.

'Hi,' says Tanya. 'Anyone else outside?' She tucks her feet in under her bum so I can sit down.

'Er, nope.' I assume she's asking if I'm an advance party. My eyes are adjusting to the gloom. Tanya's wearing a dark low-cut top that shows her bra straps and a short tight skirt. She's got a pretty smile.

Rose passes round ciggies and a bottle of Thunderbird and curls up in her armchair. 'She means her old man.' She shakes her head. 'No one there, Tanya, honest.'

'Just let him try,' Tanya says with feeling. 'Bastard.' She grins at me. 'I'm cooling off, don't mind me. I go back there now, I'd cut his sodding balls off.'

Neither of them explain further, just take swigs of Thunderbird, so after a minute I say, 'I'm on my way to Clive's. Thought I'd drop by.'

'What you done with Bethan then?' Rose asks.

'Gone with Kev.'

Rose nods several times over her ciggy. 'I like Bethan, I do. His girl,' she says to Tanya. She wags the ciggy at me. 'You got a great girl there, you know that? Best you've had. You treat her right, OK?'

Since school Rose has been telling me to treat my girlfriends right. I grin at her and pull on my cigarette.

We watch the adverts in the middle of *News at Ten*. When they end Tanya loses interest in the telly and turns to me. 'Is that Clive's in Brynmawr?' she asks. 'Party, is it?'

'Kind of. Clive's birthday.'

'Ooh, fancy a party, I do.' Tanya shivers her front with enthusiasm. Shit, I hadn't noticed before, she's got tits like torpedoes.

'Go on then,' Rose urges. 'That'd show him. Hey, he'd be mad . . .' They both start cackling and snorting like I'm not there. I'm fond of Rose but listening to them I feel my sympathies dividing.

Rose stops cackling and pushes at my knee. 'You'll take her, won't you? Just a lift. Go on. Time she had some fun.'

'Ah go on,' begs Tanya.

'Course he will,' says Rose. 'Do a favour for a mate, won't you?'

'Or a mate of a mate,' Tanya sniggers, and they both fall about again.

Seems like the decision's been made. Reckon they've been on the Thunderbird a while. I shrug and say OK. Hell, it's just a ride.

Tanya doesn't want to hang around now and once we've finished our ciggies she's up, tugging on a red fringed jacket.

Rose gets up too. 'He's got a big bike,' she says, grinning at Tanya. 'You hang on tight.'

'Ooh, I will.' Tanya gives me a coy look but I don't flatter myself I've earned it. I reckon it's free to anyone who's not her old man.

She has to nip to the lav on the way out. Rose goes in with her and I hear them whispering and giggling. Rose spends more time in lavs with girlfriends than any woman I know.

Outside the flats I give Tanya the spare helmet, start the XS, and flip the rear footrests down. Tanya clutches at the hem of her skirt and squeals, 'How'm I gonna sit on that!' But she does, I don't look round to see how. Just feel those tits ramming into my back, and her arms tight round my waist.

Rose waves us goodbye. I weave the bike back past the lock-ups, and up to the first junction.

As we round the corner I see a big bloke in singlet and tattoos striding towards us. Determined-looking fella. I've an instant intuition about him.

He stops, bellows, 'Oi!' and lunges into the road. Looks

a fit bastard too. Tanya shrieks into my left ear but I've already twisted the grip, and the bloke's just a blur in the scenery.

A hundred yards down the road I ease off and look back. He's given up on us and is making for Rose's flat. His fists are pumping at his sides.

'It's OK,' shouts Tanya in my ear. 'They get on fine, honest. I told Rose if he turned up just to tell him I've gone to Clive's.'

Oh great, I think sourly. I wonder if he knows exactly where Clive's house is. And what transport he's got. Still, nothing'll catch us over the five miles to Brynmawr.

It's a quick left and right, smart left again at the garage at the edge of town, and then we're back out on open road. Somewhere along the Whistle straight Tanya slides her hands into my jacket pockets but I reckon it's just to keep them warm. Then we're round the Racehorse Pub bends, and getting a great view of Brynmawr as we drop down off the mountain. Lit up like orange fairyland.

In the town itself we stop off at the off-licence to pick up booze. Tanya wants another bottle of Thunderbird but I say no: I won't allow glass inside jackets on my bike, and I've a cluster of fancy scars on my breastbone to remind me why. So she buys two cans of cider and I get four of Newcastle Brown.

Clive's place is only a short ride on. We turn into his road and see a small crowd on the pavement outside his house. As we trundle up I recognise Kev and Gwynfor, and yeah, the lad with the long straggly hair is Clive himself. Funny – for some reason he seems to be trying to kick his own front gate in.

I pull the bike in opposite the house, next to a GPZ that must be Jonno's. Beyond it is Gwynfor's trail bike and a few others. Tanya climbs off the XS and after I've propped it we cross the road. Looks like Kev and Gwynfor are trying to calm Clive down. Shit, I dunno; first Doggy, then Tanya, now Clive; I get the feeling I'm only a step away from trouble tonight.

'What's the gate done?' I ask Kev. Gwynfor's nearer but I'm looking for an answer this side of midnight so I pass on him. The gate's only a white wicket, looks harmless enough, but it's got Clive really riled.

'He's mad at Jonno,' says Kev. 'The bastard's done a runner. We were getting in the mood down the road,' – he nods towards the lights of a pub on the corner – 'and Jonno got us all banned. Smashing ashtrays. Tosser.'

Getting banned from your local's no joke. 'Course, it isn't Jonno's local, or Kev's, or Gwynfor's. But it is Clive's. No wonder he's steaming. The gate's holding its own, only one rail broken, you have to admire it. Mind you, most of Clive's kicks aren't connecting because he's so pissed. He's wearing a flash cowboy shirt, I notice, grey and burgundy with pearl popper studs. Bet it's a birthday present.

Clive swings round. He's just realised we've arrived.

'Where's the fucker?' he spits, weaving from side to side, as if he thinks maybe Jonno's hiding behind us. Shit, he looks wild.

'Forget him,' Kev says soothingly. He puts an arm round Clive's shoulders. 'You got a party inside. We'll sort it in the morning.'

Clive flings Kev's arm off. 'Fucker!' he bellows. He's shaking – he's going to hit someone soon, for definite. Kev's a brave lad – he's only slight but he's keeping right in there, calm as an undertaker.

Tanya's on tip-toes beside me, waving over the hedge to someone at the front window of the house. It's Marie, Clive's girlfriend. Shit, I think, remembering Tanya's old man. Looks like the girls are mates. Doubt the bloke's going to need directions.

Clive's got his fists up. Gwynfor tries to smother them in a waltzing hug but gets pushed away.

Kev sighs and says, 'You want to hit someone, Clive?'

'Fucking right I wanna hit someone,' roars Clive. 'Gonna fucking kill them.'

'Come on then.' Kev lifts his fists and squares up to him. 'Let's fight, Clivey.'

I tug Tanya back a pace. I'm not worried for Kev; he's little but he's strong, and sober. Nor for Clive, because Kev's just humouring him and won't follow anything through.

Clive takes a swing at Kev ferocious enough to lift him off his feet, but it's signposted from the start and Kev only has to step aside to take it on the shoulder padding of his jacket. Then he nips in fast while Clive's recovering and clocks him a sneaky one on the nose.

'Ah fuck,' grunts Clive. He fumbles at his face. Blood looks like gravy under street lights and there's a trickle of it oozing though his fingers.

'Mind your shirt,' says Kev quickly.

'My shirt!' wails Clive. He looks down, instantly forgetting the fight. He starts wrenching at the pearl poppers. Kev helps him get the shirt off, but it's too late. There's a couple of dark splodges down the front.

'Marie gave it me,' moans Clive.

'It's OK,' says Kev. 'We'll soak it. Cold water, no problem.' He unlatches the gate, which only sighs a little on its hinges, and steers Clive up the path towards the front door.

The rest of us follow. I hear Gwynfor introducing himself to Tanya and wonder how long it'll take her to escape. Gwynfor talks like he rides: throttle set on drone, only brakes when the road runs out.

Kev takes Clive into the kitchen to soak the shirt and the rest of us go through to the sitting room. Bethan's on the sofa chatting to Marie; Jaz and Mitch and a few others are over by the drinks. Jaz is rolling a party joint on the table with a dozen skins. I prop myself on the arm of the sofa and tap Bethan on the shoulder with a beer can.

She looks up, smiles, 'Oh, hi, great,' and swivels to take the can. 'You heard? We all got booted out the pub. Because of that prat Jonno. Clive's raving.'

'Yeah,' I say, snapping open a can myself. 'I know.' I take a swig. Bethan's in jeans and a black shirt, knotted at the front. You can tell she's Kev's sister. Same small neat shape, same easy calm about her. I want to sink on to the sofa beside her but I can't, with Tanya's old man on my mind.

It looks like Tanya's only just detached herself from Gwynfor's life history. She's pretending to admire bike rally stickers by the window but really she's keeping an eye out.

Reluctantly I push myself up from the sofa and walk over to her.

'Waiting for your old man?' I say over her shoulder.

She glances back at me with a quick smile. I reckon she's regretting coming here already.

'Who's he going to be mad at?' I ask. 'You or me?'

She dips her smile. 'You, maybe. But he don't know you. I won't let on.'

'Would he know the bike?' I ask. I'd heal, but the XS wouldn't.

She thinks. 'Doubt it. Dark, wasn't it. Not to be sure, anyways.'

'What's he drive?'

'Red pick-up.'

I nod, and decide not to move the bike.

Clive comes in barechested with Kev behind him. Marie jumps up crying, 'Where's your shirt?' and Kev assures her it's fine, hanging clean as new, just a bit wetter, over the bath. Clive's nose looks puffy and he's still breathing heavy but Jaz has just finished constructing the twelve-skin spliff and presents it to him with a flourish. Kev offers a light and we all sing a round of *Happy Birthday to you* as Clive gets the joint glowing. That'll mellow him some.

When the singing's over Kev takes me to one side.

'Don't let Jonno in if he comes back. Don't want Clive set off again.'

'You expecting him?'

'Has to get his bike some time. Depends if he's still mad. Clive clipped him one outside the pub.'

I glance over at Tanya, and tell Kev we might have another visitor, and why.

'Shit,' murmurs Kev. He thinks about it and then shrugs. 'Just don't let him near Clive. Sort it outside, OK?'

I nod and return to Tanya, who's still gazing out the window.

'If he turns up, how 'bout you going out to him?' I say. 'Clive's a bit wound up. You want to go back with him, don't you?'

She pulls a face, then sighs and says, 'Suppose so. Yeah.' She points at the window. 'There is someone out there. Not me old man, but some bloke. Across the road.'

I take a look. A big-shouldered lad in a leather jacket is standing by the bikes. Shaved head, fleshy face, long black-and-white tasselled scarf.

'It's Jonno.' Shit, I think. Doesn't look as if he's planning an entrance though. He's trying to pull his GPZ out from the other bikes. But making a mess of it because he's so pissed. Only a pillock like Jonno would try to ride his bike rat-arsed. He pulls the GPZ a yard out of the line, then seems to give up and lets it roll back. He digs around in his pockets, swaying as he rummages. He's found a packet of fags and lighting up. For a moment he seems to be thinking mighty thoughts, face tilted skywards, pulling on the ciggy. Then he recollects himself, works his way out from the bikes and starts walking towards the house.

'Tell Kev,' I say quickly to Tanya. 'Discreet like.' I'm already moving to the door.

I let myself out the front and close the door behind me. Jonno's trying to open the garden gate but it's sulking now and refusing to let him in. He punches it, swearing, jettisons his ciggy, and starts to climb over it.

'Oi!' I call. 'No need to bother. Just piss off, OK.'

'Where's that fucker Clive?' Jonno says thickly. There's a sound of cracking wood as he makes it over the gate. That's another strut gone. Hell, I sigh, walking down to him, and I'm a peace-loving bloke.

I grasp him by his upper arm and swing him round so he's pointing back the way he's come. There's nothing wrong with the gate latch – Jonno just never found it – so I lift it and yank the gate wide. Behind us I hear the front door open – it's Kev and Tanya. I try to push Jonno out on to the pavement but he's seen the others and they're distracting him.

'You get Clive,' he shouts over his shoulder at them. 'Tell him Jonno's here.'

Kev runs down to us and together we shove him through the gate. He's flailing around but nothing purposeful.

'Go home, Jonno,' hisses Kev. 'Clive don't want to see you.'

'Get his keys first,' I say. 'He was trying to pull his bike out.'

We both try to find the keys but leather jackets have too many pockets and Jonno's dead set against the idea, swearing and hitting us off.

We're still wrestling with him as headlights approach

from down the road. Double headlights, high and wide. We stop wrestling. Oh shit, I think. Could be a pick-up.

It is a pick-up. A red one. It pulls up twenty yards away and the driver jumps out. The bloke's got a denim jacket on now over his singlet and he's so keen to say hello he leaves the driver's door swinging wide.

Kev, Jonno and I watch him approach, kind of mesmerised. Kev and I because we know who he is and our brains are log-jammed, and Jonno because he's so pissed it's his resting state anyway.

Suddenly Tanya's between me and Jonno. She's slipping her arm around Jonno's waist. Planting a big kiss on his ugly mug. Kev and I come to our senses at the same time, twig what she's doing, and step away. Ooh you clever girl, I think.

Jonno's overjoyed to be so irresistible, flinging his arms around Tanya and trying to stick his tongue in her ear. Such spontaneous affection, it's a pleasure to watch. Even Tanya's old man is smiling. Kind of.

Tanya wriggles away from Jonno, says, 'Ta for a lovely evening,' and skips off towards the pick-up.

Tanya's old man stands with his legs braced in front of Jonno, glares at him, and then wallops him a backhander across the face. Jonno never saw it coming and looks surprised more than hurt. So the bloke belts him again and this time Jonno's legs give way and he's down, hard, on his bum. I feel a mite sorry for him, sitting there looking dull on the pavement, but if anyone deserves it he does, and Tanya's old man has come a long way to get satisfaction. It's not his fault he's got the wrong lad.

Kev's tensing, just in case the bloke's a psycho, but I'm fairly sure he's not, and I'm right: he backs off, lifting his palms to us, and says, 'Personal matter, boys. No offence.'

Kev relaxes, and I nod and say, 'None taken.' While Jonno's still wondering who cut his legs off Kev squats down beside him, digs around in his pockets, and finds the bike keys. So Tanya's old man's done Jonno a favour really – he won't be killing himself or anyone else driving home. Done favours all round, in fact.

The bloke strolls back to his pick-up. I can see Tanya inside the cab and she don't look scared. Scared women don't titivate in driving mirrors. Reckon we don't need to worry about her.

The pick-up roars off up the road. We try to get Jonno on his feet but he's lost interest in being vertical and twists away from us. He pats at the pavement as if it's a lumpy mattress and tries to get his head down. Nothing like a near view of the floor when you're pissed to make you want to stay there. But we can't leave him on the pavement so Kev nips down to his van, reverses it up close, and we heave him into the back. Jonno curls up cosy on the carpet and he's snoring like a two-stroke before we get the back doors closed.

Kev parks the van down the road again and we tramp back into the house. Metallica's on the stereo and the air's sweet and thick. Clive's so mellow now he's fast asleep on the carpet in front of the fireplace. A friendly arm-wrestling contest's going on down the room and Marie and another girl are dancing by the window, heads on each other's shoulders, movements slow and boozy.

I finally get to sink down next to Bethan on the sofa, snap open another beer can, and start mellowing out myself.

ABERRANCE IN THE
EMOTIONAL SPECTRUM

At first we thought we had a problem with the COS viewer. Then with the subject under study – and this must be the case. All the same, it indicates a limitation in the equipment we haven't run across before.

For those not in psychotherapeutic or law enforcement circles, I should explain that the COS viewer is a device, still in development but already in use, capable of displaying human emotions as colours. The acronym stands for Canine Olfactory Spectrometer, though canine material hasn't actually been used since the prototype days; the name has stuck because of its descriptive power. (Most people are aware that dogs possess olfactory organs thousands of times more sensitive than their human equivalents, and that dogs can virtually 'see' smells.) The machine is constructed to ignore normally detectable odours but to pick up the tiny organic emissions associated with emotional states and reveal these through the viewer, which resembles a bulky camera. Because the machine 'sees' the emissions as coloured light, the actual organic content does not have to impact on the receptor (the associated 'light' radiation is enough) which means the device can be used not only through unobstructed air, but also through glass or other transparencies. Use of the machine requires a high level of skill – our partnership, for instance, consists of a psychologist (myself) and a behaviour analyst (my colleague Felicity) – but the benefits are huge. It has added immeasurably to our arsenal of interpretive techniques. The Derek and Felicity team has, on numerous occasions, saved lives.

One of the most fascinating findings, discovered early on in the research, is that the colours seen by us through the COS viewer bear close parallels to colours accepted linguistically across the world as being associated with particular emotions. This suggests that these colours, though invisible to the naked human eye, are nonetheless subliminally registered – possibly by our own deficient olfactory organs – and that this 'intuitive' perception has influenced language.

White or yellow, for instance, is emitted at times of fear. Of the two, white is the easier to interpret, though the harder, in our line of work, to deal with. It indicates the emotion of pure fear. We are very careful with subjects emitting bright white, as extreme fear is a stupefying emotion, and subjects emitting bright white are prone to irrationality and to sudden, often dangerously impulsive actions. They require calm handling and intense reassurance before anything more constructive can take place. Yellow, whether bright or pale, is easier to work with. Yellow, in language, is associated with cowardice, and you can see how this has arisen, but we see it as an unhelpful interpretation. In our view, yellow indicates a level and type of fear where rational thought and judgement are still operating. Where, that is, the subject can see the way ahead, but is too frightened, *just at this moment*, to take it. We can work productively on yellow.

Black is the colour of anger. (Yes, black, in the emotional spectrum, unlike in the light spectrum, is a 'colour' in its own right.) We are careful with subjects emitting black too, though our responses may be more active and dynamic. Over a variable length of time black tends to fade, like newsprint, to grey. Grey is the colour of depression, grief, sadness, hopelessness. It is actually easier to tackle black-emitters than grey-emitters, because black-emitters are more alert and more amenable to communication. Grey-emitters are frustratingly poor listeners and can be highly resistant to suggestion or advice. As Felicity puts it – and this is a statement of fact, not an unkindness – 'the losers have given up'. However, as long as they remain grey, and don't suddenly flash over into black, they are usually dangers only to themselves.

Red, which is the colour of both guilt and shame (they're not the same, of course, but the viewer isn't refined enough to distinguish between them), we see only rarely. People ask if this colour is more prevalent in women than in men, because women, it is often said, are 'better' at feeling guilt, but this hasn't been our experience. I, for instance, have been known to emit bursts of red, but Felicity never! Perhaps men make up for lower levels of guilt with higher levels of shame. In any case, most of our work subjects, at the time we're viewing them, are not red-emitters. That, very often, is precisely their problem.

We are more likely, indeed, to see blue-emitters. Blue is what all of us emit when we are 'unemotional', 'relaxed' or, paradoxically, 'concentrating' – presumably because our minds, at times of concentration, are too occupied to be emotional. Blue is particularly strongly seen just before sleep, or immediately after the cessation of severe pain. It can be induced by meditative techniques. There is a yogi we have tested who emits blue almost perpetually, an amazing and rather chilling sight. The blue-emitter subjects we see at work are vaguely chilling too, because the colour indicates a mood totally inappropriate to the occasion. However, blue-emitters retain full powers of intellect – many are alarmingly and deviously clever – and are usually open to argument, especially if this can be couched so as to appeal to their strong sense of self-interest.

Green can indicate envy, as it is used metaphorically in language, but, when it does, is a very yellow green. That kind of envy, we suspect, must contain an element of past, unconquered fear. It is the begrudgement of others for what one feels one could have achieved oneself, if one had been more courageous. For those who could not possibly hope to have achieved what is envied, but are still in the grip of a powerful 'envious' emotion, the colour emitted is more likely to be black. Anger, that is. There is some difference among psychologists regarding green, but personally I associate it with bitterness, and, where it veers more towards turquoise, which bright green can decay to over time, with cynicism.

The colour of happiness, it surprises most people to learn, is not a pure, primary, jolly colour. Nor is it the colour of sunrises, or verdant pastures, or brilliant starshine. It is, in fact, brown. Indeed, all positive emotions fall somewhere in the brown range. My own view is that in true euphoria all emotional charges are released simultaneously, in a kind of ecstatic explosion, and it is this combined surge that gives us the brownish emission, as well as the inner sense of feeling gloriously 'whole'.

I have only once seen a strong brown-emitter while at work, and this subject had, until the very last minute, been one of the very rare red-emitters. He was impossible to negotiate with, because he clearly wanted the release of death – he had just killed his wife and at the time was seriously threatening his children – and he was, I would say, a deeply tortured individual. He became a brown-emitter in the last few seconds before the police shot him. He had arranged himself in a brightly lit window as a clear, easy target, and that was when the emission began. I told the marksman responsible this, and possibly it helped him in his debriefing.

Love and hate, despite being categorized in the textbooks as sentiments rather than emotions, still have colour emissions associated with them. These emissions, however, are more directional – ie, they are aimed at something – and they occur as flashes, very often, rather than as the glows of all-pervading moods. Having said that, hate, at least, seems a remarkably durable emotion; it's been our experience that hate towards a particular other may persist indefinitely, even if it is activated only for short bursts at a time; while anger, say, with which hate is often associated, seems to break down to depression (grey), bitterness (green), or some other emotion relatively quickly. The colour of hate is a deep, dark, consistent purple, one of the richest and most easily detectable colours in the emotional spectrum. The colour of love, on the other hand, is neither consistent nor uniform, suggesting that the sentiment itself is more complex. Its colour is generally a shade of warm brown (it falls, naturally, within the euphoric range) but often includes flickers of pale white (suggesting anxiety), sometimes flashes of black (fierceness, or aggression?) and sometimes a soft dove grey (pain, sadness, longing?). Sometimes, under all this 'interference' from other colours, the warm brown background is almost swamped out. We rarely see it while we're at work.

I have oversimplified the above in the interests of clarity; in real life human beings, especially highly stressed human beings, as our subjects tend to be, are often in the grip of – and thus emitting the colours of – more than one emotion, and these emotions may be conflicting. Oscillation

between emotions is also common. This is why the interpretation of COS images requires great skill. But although
we as operators have sometimes found ourselves defeated
by the more complex colour patterns, and have had to fall
back on more traditional interpretive techniques (which,
when unsighted, we of course do anyway) we have
always, when using the viewer, had material to work with.
Up till now.

Our problem is that we now have a subject – Subject A,
I'll call him – who, for significant periods (up to 43 minutes,
so far) emits nothing detectable through the COS viewer
at all. This is unprecedented. The only zero recordings
previously encountered have been those of sleeping subjects
(when not in REM phases) or of unconscious or catatonic
subjects. Subject A, however, is indisputably conscious, not
remotely catatonic, and yet still, from time to time, registers
nothing.

At first – while we were still on site – we thought we had
an intermittent fault in the viewer. Our resourceful young
technician, Peter, had managed to install a receptor right
inside the building, so we were able to train it on Subject A
almost constantly during the negotiations, and our natural
assumption when the viewer blanked was that we had a
fault. The machine can't pick up anything except emotional
discharge, so in its absence all you get is a fuzzy nothing-
ness, like a television picture with the aerial disconnected.
However, we did notice that when the hostage was in frame
we regained normal reception – brilliant white face and
hands, poor lad, with a stripe down the front indicating an
open shirt or jacket – and back at the station we experimented
further. Subject A still had periods of non-emission, but
when, during one of these, the viewer was switched to
another subject (Felicity) a normal picture immediately
returned. (Felicity is always willing to be guinea pig, probably

because she habitually emits shades of blue, which she attributes to a naturally relaxed disposition and the absence of a punitive super-ego. It's generous of her to volunteer so often; she knows I dislike being viewed. If we're alone I'm not so reluctant, but with others, Peter say, especially if she is giving him attention, I find it hard to suppress emissions of jealousy (green) or dislike (pale purple). It is our little joke.)

This control observation has, anyway, ruled out a glitch in the machinery. Felicity wonders if extreme psychopathy – and Subject A does exhibit profound psychopathic traits – might be the cause. Perhaps some psychopaths are capable of, quite simply, feeling nothing. I would be happier with this explanation if we had come across it before. We deal with psychopaths regularly in this job and, in my experience, while they are capable of emitting any colour except red, their 'resting' colour, as it were, tends to be blue. That is, when not provoked or stimulated to other reactions, they tend to calmness. I have met several who, under the most appallingly tense circumstances, nevertheless gave all the COS appearance of being smugly at ease with themselves. (Note: the fact that Felicity is commonly a blue-emitter does not mean that she has psychopathic tendencies! In her case, being a professional, a relaxed unemotional calmness is entirely appropriate.)

Luckily we now have Subject A safely in custody and since he is apparently delighted to be the focus of so much scientific attention, we hope, with his cooperation, to get to the truth. We have followed our usual work pattern: Felicity has been through the files and prepared a case study, while I have been picking up what I can from observing interviews with the released hostage and witnesses. (I know Felicity feels that occasionally these roles should be reversed, but her skills at scanning files

and wordprocessing reports are far superior to mine –
women seem to have a natural aptitude for keyboarding –
and my observational talents, with fifteen years more
clinical experience, far exceed hers. Each to their own. If
push came to shove – which of course it never would – I
am, in any case, by virtue of seniority, the higher ranking
officer.)

Felicity's report doesn't make pleasant reading. Subject A
is what, in common parlance, one would call a sex maniac.
His victims are young men, preferably *uniformed* young
men (Felicity cleverly spotted this connection – what an
eye for detail), who he invites back to his house and then is
unwilling to release. He is a physically intimidating man
with a controlling, gloating manner that terrifies his
victims, but he is not gratuitously violent. He does not
sexually assault the young men but humiliates them by
satisfying himself sexually in their presence. The longest
he has detained a victim (as far as we know) has been six
days, after which the young man was released distressed
but not seriously harmed. Since his latest victim, like
previous victims, accompanied him home freely, he is not
being charged with kidnapping or abduction, but with
ABH (this victim tried with some determination to leave
and got knocked about a bit) and false imprisonment. We
know a lot about Subject A because he is already on file –
there have been complaints before, though none, due
to the reluctance of victims to press charges, came to
anything – and because the man himself is remarkably
cooperative in interview. According to my own researches,
the young man we released today met Subject A two nights
ago in a club where the clientele dress up in outrageous
'fancy dress' outfits. The victim was wearing a uniform (of
a tasteless stormtrooper type) and for this reason attracted
Subject A's attention. Luckily the young man was with

friends before he was persuaded to depart with Subject A, and these friends not only reported him missing the next day, but could also give us a very accurate description of the man he had left with. In all fairness I should say that these friends come across as entirely normal individuals, living very ordinary, respectable, daytime lives. The young victim himself is a hospital nurse. Twenty years ago, when I was their age, any desire to dress up in flagrantly kinky clothes – whatever one's sexual orientation – would have been satisfied behind drawn domestic curtains, not paraded in public places. I made this observation to Felicity, and she retorted that lack of guilt or shame about such things are healthy developments and make the world a much safer place. I bow to her opinion. For the young man in question, given that the speed of his release was entirely due to the unembarrassed frankness of his friends, she must certainly be right.

Thinking about this has made me realize that we have never before dealt with a serious sex offender. As negotiators and interpreters Felicity and I deal with a range of individuals, but our commonest subjects are aggrieved, desperate husbands or partners, and holed-up villains. I cannot recall attending a single past siege involving a sex offender who was using his victim as hostage. (Which is not to say that hostages are not now and again sexually assaulted by their captors, but there is a difference.) I can also not recall a case before where the captor has treated the incident – even before apprehension and arrest – with such levity, almost as if he were enjoying it. Perhaps he was, though the COS viewer rarely displayed brown hues. Instead, at those times when Subject A, viewed with the naked eye or through a camera, appeared closest to showing pleasure, it simply went blank.

We have now sent Subject A upstairs to the FME to be medically examined and to have samples of his blood and urine taken. (We are considering the possibility that he has some physical peculiarity or biochemical imbalance that blocks certain emissions.) In the meantime Felicity and I are taking a long-overdue break in the staff canteen. This break would be more enjoyable if Peter hadn't joined us; he has an annoying habit of calling Felicity 'Fliss', and is in my opinion presumptuously over-familiar with her. Felicity does not encourage him but nor does she slap him down, which really she would be wise to; this station takes a dim view of male-female friendships across ranks. However, I know she would be sharp with me if I remonstrated with him on her behalf – she is a very modern woman – so I have to pretend to ignore him. One of the things we have been discussing, very much not for the first time, is how much easier our task would be if COS readings could be recorded. The fact that they can't be is why each COS operation requires the attendance of two interpreters, since it is unreasonable to expect one person to be permanently glued to the eyepiece. Not that I'd be without Felicity, of course, but neither of us comes cheap. The chance to rerun observations, too, would be enormously helpful. In this case, for instance, having established that the 'visual silences' were not due to machine error, we could have rerun all the episodes, and perhaps spotted common precipitating factors. However, although the time will soon come – all that's needed, Peter says, is a device to transform the signals into ones that register on magnetic tape – it has not arrived yet. Notes and memory are all very well, but neither can record everything.

We have been invited up to have a word with the FME, who has completed his examination. Subject A is now back in the cells. Peter wanted to come too but I discouraged him – interpretation is not a technician's business – and he took the hint. The FME says Subject A is a healthy, normal 38-year-old in all physical respects that he can determine, though of course we will have to wait for the blood and urine analysis to confirm this. He does, however, have one very interesting observation to make. Subject A, he says, gives all the appearance of being in a state of permanent sexual arousal. Body flush, pupil enlargement, the lot. The taking of a urine sample, he says, was anything but the quick, simple procedure it usually is. He is a clever man, the FME, and before examining Subject A had done his homework by reading Felicity's case notes. It is his opinion that it was the presence of the escort constable that was exciting Subject A (because his state of arousal visibly heightened when the officer was in view) and he suggests that Subject A is finding the whole situation, the whole experience of being surrounded by men in uniforms (as one is, both in a siege situation and in a police station) intensely gratifying.

There is an obvious conclusion to be drawn from this. It surprises me; I had somehow imagined that in a state of acute arousal the emotions would be very forceful. And, as emissions, strongly, powerfully brown – the culmination of acute arousal, orgasm, is surely the ultimate in euphoria. But perhaps, if you view the state as an inward-turned, self-centred, black-hole sort of event, one that sucks in, rather then emits outward . . . the words *consumed with lust* suggest themselves . . . or, indeed, see orgasm as a release of a quite different order to emotional release, involving experience and feeling quite beyond the normal range . . .

My goodness. The ramifications could be stupendous. My brain is jumping with possibilities. But first things first. We must, absolutely must, attempt to repeat the observation. As soon as possible. And not with Subject A – that would prove nothing.

I wonder if Peter would help. Felicity has returned to the canteen to tell him about the doctor's findings. It's not something you could properly ask of an outsider, but Peter would see a request in the right light, surely, since he has shown himself just as keen as us to investigate the anomaly. I'm sure I haven't seen anything about orgasmic COS emissions, or lack of them, in the literature. Preliminary results, even based on a very ad hoc experiment, would be of great interest to a lot of people – not just COS interpreters. I can see an article in it already. Perhaps several. And how difficult would it be to arrange? We could do it here. Peter and a few rude magazines in Interview 6 (the room with the one-way glass) and me with the COS viewer next door. If I promised to keep my eyes on the viewer eyepiece until it was over, it would even be relatively unembarrassing, since he wouldn't have to face the viewer and, if we were proved right, would actually disappear for the crucial moments.

On the other hand, in his shoes, I wouldn't do it. But this may just be because I couldn't contemplate either Peter or Felicity in the next room. Felicity because she is a woman; and Peter because, frankly, I don't trust him. It's not that I think he'd actually do anything improper (what, short of inviting his friends in, could count as 'improper'?) but I do think that these sort of experiments have to be conducted in an atmosphere of trust. These sorts of experiments especially. Otherwise, among other things, one can imagine performance difficulties. But I doubt lack of trust would be a problem for Peter. We may not be bosom buddies, but I'm sure he has never doubted my professionalism.

It is a great shame that COS pictures can't be recorded. I had a kind of flash fantasy then, of myself and Felicity, alone in a room with a recording viewer . . .

And that disgraceful thought raises a further point. I

wonder, if men's emotional side really is put on hold, swamped out, or perhaps implodes, at times of intense lustfulness or arousal, is the same true for women? This question will doubtless have already occurred to Felicity – she is very hot on the female perspective. On the other hand it's not a question we could investigate immediately, as we would need to draft in a fully briefed female volunteer, since Felicity, for propriety's sake, would have to man (or rather woman!) the viewer. But we could settle the male question straight away. I think, while my enthusiasm is high, and we are all still on the premises, I will find Felicity and discuss it with her.

We have had a long talk. I am not at all – *at all* – happy with the outcome, in fact I am deeply *un*happy. However, I know that if I refuse to go along with what Felicity proposes she will take umbrage, and probably accuse me of questioning her professionalism. She has already suggested that my reluctance is bound up with my personal feelings towards her, which I automatically denied, though of course she is right. Her argument is that, if we do as she proposes, we will kill two birds with one stone, as it were, need to involve no one outside the team, and will obtain the results we want (hopefully) very fast. The only counter arguments I have actually articulated are that *(a)* her way is bound to be very much more indecorous and embarrassing for the participants, and *(b)* that all research shows that women can bring themselves to orgasm very much faster through masturbation than in the act of intercourse. To the first she scoffed, 'Really, Derek, we're scientists, embarrassment doesn't come into it,' and to the second she replied, 'So what?' She went on to point out that while a man might be able to set the ball rolling with dirty magazines, the same was not true for women (or for herself, anyway) and that the attentions of an attractive male, with whom she already has a bond of friendship and trust, would be much more likely to achieve results. And then she said, 'It's not as if the whole world will be watching, Derek. Only you.'

A small crumb of comfort in all this is that Peter apparently also took some persuading. He goes up, marginally, in my estimation. He has agreed only after reminders that COS images are grossly undefined, compared to camera images, that, if the experiment goes as we expect, they will both be invisible to me for at least some of the time (as long as I keep my eyes on the viewer eyepiece) and, of course, that the images are unrecordable. I have a strong suspicion that both Peter and I are being bullied into agreement by a spurious logic employed for dubious ends, but those ends will achieve ours too, and so, despite our – or at least my – deep reservations, Felicity has got her way.

They have removed the table from the interview room and borrowed a clean mattress from the rape suite storeroom (there has to be irony in that) which they have laid out on the floor. I have lined up the COS viewer next door and tested it through the glass. Peter is currently emitting yellows and whites, interspersed with bursts of brown, i.e. he is oscillating between acute anxiety and anticipation, while Felicity is emitting her usual blue, with occasional flashes of rich brown. These seem particularly strong when her body – and so possibly her gaze – turns to the one-way glass, which I find vaguely disconcerting.

The deed is done. It's a good thing I haven't had a COS viewer trained on me. I imagine the results would have been a whirling kaleidoscope of colours, none of them remotely brown. Greens and blacks, I suspect, in the main. Flashes of purple, too, very possibly, as the experiment progressed.

Felicity, at the start, lost her brown flashes and became exclusively blue. Concentrating on reassuring Peter, I guessed. He slowly lost his whites and yellows, and by the time he was naked (you can't see the clothes, of course, but you can see the emergence of coloured flesh) he had become consistently brown. Then more of Felicity became visible – turning brown too – and their shapes became excruciatingly active. I haven't watched naked bodies through the machine since the very early development days, and – obviously, otherwise we wouldn't be doing this – never bodies preparing for sexual intercourse. The images are quite defined enough to stir intense feelings of voyeurism – at several points I had to force myself not to pull away from the eyepiece. But then, just as I was wondering how much more I could possibly take, Felicity's glowing brown shape simply faded away. This should have caused a surge of brown emissions from me, given what we had set out to prove, but I am absolutely sure it didn't. Indeed, I clicked on the 'Felicity' stop watch with such violence I'm surprised I didn't damage it. Peter remained visible for only a few seconds before he too vanished. I clicked the second stopwatch. I don't know which was worse, being able to see them, or not being able to. I remained watching what appeared to be a blank screen for some considerable time (which additionally enraged me – there was no need for them to spin it out) before Peter reappeared (I clicked his watch off) followed a minute or so later by Felicity (hers off too). Felicity emerged a deep rich blue, interspersed with pulses of pale brown, while Peter was a uniform warm rich brown, which, over the time I continued to watch them, showed no sign of fading. I fear he may be a sentimentalist, the silly man.

I removed my eyes from the viewer once I was sure they were dressed and upright. Felicity, through the one-way glass, looked her usual neat business-like self, though, in my opinion, suspiciously bright-eyed, while Peter looked idiotically tousled and sheepish. In a moment of spite I toyed with the idea of reporting that no visual silences had occurred at all, but decided that the implications of this would dismay Peter far more than Felicity, who would probably just find it funny. And the lie would be bound to be exposed at a later date, since we're not the only people using these machines. Anyway, look at what we had just proved – hardly the moment to consider professional suicide.

However, I do not think I can continue to work with a woman like Felicity. I had no idea – really, not an inkling – that she disliked me so much. 'All in the name of science, Derek,' she has just said to me, her voice so offhand and airy that I felt a powerful urge to strangle her. Does she think I'm stupid? Does she think I can't see through her? No; the answer, of course, is that she knows exactly how obvious her motives are to me – I am, after all, a highly skilled interpreter – but she simply doesn't care. The manipulative cleverness of the blue-emitter. Two birds with one stone, as she said before we started: she has punished me (for whatever crimes I have apparently committed) and indulged her lust for Peter; and yet remains herself, entirely – and in the eyes of the world, even courageously – above reproach. I shall definitely request a transfer. My eyes are now truly open. The woman is a menace to her colleagues. What a tramp.

ONE DAY

William stood at the centre of the small empty beach, staring out to sea, the yellow-stone hotel façade behind him. The early-morning August air was not yet hot; even so, he unbuttoned his shirt, slipped it off, and tied the arms loosely around his hips. He felt his naked skin tighten and prickle in the breeze. He walked, slowly, the short length of the cove, and then back again. A few years ago, when his hotel duties had been less onerous, he would have swum now. As a teenager, every day in the season, weather permitting. These days the short walk on the beach, the exposure of his skin to the sea air, was more ritual than true relaxation. Just something he did every day at quarter to eight, before the guests were up, shaking off the previous intense hour of office work.

The exercise was nonetheless invigorating. At the top of the beach he left the sand and bounded up the wide steps to the hotel terrace. And once there he was immediately dragged back to duty by the untidiness of the flower displays in the concrete urns along the frontage. None of the annuals deadheaded, the packed compost inside each doormat dry. Getting competent staff and keeping them, such a distance from town, was a permanent problem. Guests came to the hotel for the quiet solitude, the inaccessibility, of the place.

Staff were reluctant to stay, or even travel in daily, for the same reasons. He unrolled a length of hose from its wheel, turned the outside tap on, and started to gush water into the urns.

As he was flooding the last, a voice behind him said, 'William?' The tall, aproned shape of his mother leant from the open staff door, her hands pressed against the jambs either side.

'It's me,' William said. 'Just watering the tubs. D'you need something?'

The sun on the thick lenses of his mother's spectacles made them look opaque. Usually, in morning light, and before her eyes grew tired, she could see well enough to recognize him. But perhaps she was dazzled.

'Grapefruit juice,' his mother said. 'Sorry, dear. Two guests have just come down. They'd prefer it.'

'Right,' said William. 'Be along now.'

His mother withdrew. William frowned. Why couldn't his mother find the grapefruit juice? As always, any indication that her sight might be deteriorating further caused a flicker of alarm, along with a flicker of something deeper: a kind of alertness, almost an excitement. Accompanied by a tiny shameful voice that whispered: *one day, one day*. He turned off the tap and rerolled the hose – guests could fall over anything – and went inside. His mother never usually involved him in breakfast. She laid it out in hot dishes on the dining-room sideboard, from which guests helped themselves. The regime worked well; there was more waste than with waitress service, but much less work involved. His mother could still cook, magnificently – her food, as much as the idyllic location, was the hotel's main asset – but could no longer serve at table.

He opened one of the larder fridges. The juice cartons were in the door, obvious, surely, even to his mother; what she had been unable to work out, he realized, was the difference between grapefruit and orange, when the undecorated packs were unopened and she couldn't use her nose.

Relieved, he broke open a carton of grapefruit and poured it into a jug. Then discarded the crumpled shirt from his hips and put on a clean white chef's shirt from the pile beside the cooking range.

'Which guests?' he asked. He didn't say, 'Shall I take it through for you?' because his mother disliked reminders of what she couldn't do.

'Mrs Jennings and her sister.' His mother was good at voices. She was preparing picnic boxes on the stainless steel work table behind him. Her movements at this sort of job were so deft and competent that no stranger entering the room would have guessed at her disability.

He carried the jug through to the dining room. Mrs Jennings – Katherine Jennings, she had entered herself in the register, with a defiant flourish – had been here earlier in the season with her husband and two young children, and had returned yesterday with her sister Geraldine. Geraldine was a darker, more compact, quicker-eyed version of Katherine. The only other occupants of the dining room were the Clayton family over by the window: mother, father, and six-form age daughter.

'Oh, wonderful!' Katherine Jennings cried, as William approached their table. 'Personal service. We are honoured.' Her sister gave a snort of amusement.

'No trouble at all,' he said, smiling at both of them. 'I'll make sure there's some out for you tomorrow.'

'Great. And William – it is William, isn't it?' She glanced across at her sister.

'It is.'

'Have you got any sunbeds for the terrace? We fancied a lazy morning.'

'Of course,' said William. 'I'll put some out for you.'

He moved on to check the Claytons were happy. While standing over their table – of course they were happy, everything was quite marvellous – he avoided their daughter's gaze. William tended to ignore very young women. Young women were uncomfortable reminders that in another, less responsible, less dutiful life, they would have been his companions, friends, lovers. This girl was, what, seventeen, eighteen? He was twenty-four. The same generation; but it was a generation from which he felt irrevocably excluded.

He was aware, as he took leave of the family, that the two older women at the other table were silent and motionless. Eyes on each other, waiting for him to leave the room. As he did, he caught their upper bodies moving toward each other, heard the first hiss and giggle. He wondered briefly about them. Flirts could operate in pairs; serious adventurers, probably not. William did, just occasionally, run across serious adventurers. Holidaying women off the leash, off the beaten track, determined to enjoy themselves. Usually women in their late twenties, thirties – the sisters were both well into their thirties – past the age of shyness, or romantic notions. Of course he never pursued them; but he did, just occasionally, find himself pursued. He was perceived, he guessed, as a safe, discreet, uncomplicated target. Rightly perceived. Over the years, with diminishing guilt, he had slept with several such women. There was no real crime in it. He was a young man. With the hours he worked, opportunities were few enough.

He returned outside to unchain a nest of sun loungers from the lean-to at the far end of the terrace and laid several out across the stone flags. Then went back to his office behind the reception desk to finish off the paperwork he had started before his stroll. He kept the door open, so he could be seen by passing guests. After twenty minutes or so he was interrupted by a tentative, 'Hello?' It was Mr and Mrs Clayton. He went out to greet them.

'We're off for the day,' said Mrs Clayton. They were carrying two of his mother's picnic boxes. 'I hope you don't mind, but Fiona would prefer to stay here.' She laughed, adult to adult, as if he were nearer their age than their daughter's. 'The beach, sunbathing, you know . . .'

'That's perfectly all right,' William said. The Claytons, he guessed, were not regular hotel-goers. Used to bed and breakfast stays. 'She must do as she pleases.'

The Claytons looked relieved and grateful. He saw them off, tidied up the last of his paperwork, and returned to the staff quarters to check the two cleaners had arrived – by taxi, at the hotel's expense – and then consulted with his mother about the evening menu and the fruit and vegetables required. When he emerged with a list he found the Claytons' daughter – Fiona, her parents had called her – in shorts and skimpy halterneck top, hesitating outside the kitchen door.

'Can I help you?' He could hardly ignore her here. She had a smooth, un-madeup face, her hair scraped back into a neat French plait.

'Ah, well, yes.' Her expression was friendly, undaunted. 'A cup of coffee would be nice.'

'Of course,' he said. 'Where would you like it? There are sunbeds on the terrace.'

'Oh, terrific.' She smiled gratefully at him as he directed her through the lounge.

When he took the coffee out she was lying on her back on one of the sunbeds, alone – no sign yet of Katherine or Geraldine. Her limbs were straight and slender. He felt a familiar ache, standing over her.

She sat up. In a small rush, as if she had been rehearsing the words, she said, 'Do you mind if I ask you something?'

'Fire away.' The colloquialism just slipped out. As if she wasn't a guest at all.

'Are you the manager of this hotel?'

'I am indeed. And owner.'

Her eyes became circles. 'Owner? Wow!'

He smiled. 'Along with my mother, and, of course, the bank.'

'Your mother – have I seen her?'

'The cook.'

'Oh, the amazing food. Sorry . . . I know this sounds nosy, but I'm starting a course next month, in hotel management. I was going to ask you how you got into it, but . . .'

'I was born into it,' William said. 'I've never known anything else.'

'God.' Fiona looked at him with wonder. 'You could tell me lots . . .'

He had errands to do. The fruit and vegetable list. And young women, he always told himself, were painful company. All the same.

'I'd love to. But right now I have to go out. Unless . . .' He hesitated. He denied himself pleasure, to avoid the pain. The promise of pleasure was suddenly overriding. He didn't want to suggest anything of which her parents would disapprove, but they saw him as a responsible adult, didn't they? And he was a responsible adult. 'You can come with me, if you like. See what I get up to.'

'Shadow you? Wow!' Her expression, as she swung her legs off the sunbed, gulping at the coffee, was astonished, delighted. She was genuinely interested. She was not flirting. He was not flirting. He would, quite simply, show her what he did.

In the white hotel van he told her to call him William. She asked where his father was, if he worked here too, and he told her that his father had died a few years ago, and that was why he was now the manager. She didn't say, 'Oh, I'm sorry,' just nodded, as if a few years was a lifetime ago, and said she was eighteen, nearly nineteen, and couldn't wait to leave home and start college.

'We're going to an organic farm,' he explained, as he drove the van inland. 'Meat and fish are delivered, but vegetables we buy in daily. At the farm we can choose exactly what we want. This isn't really a manager's job,' he stressed. 'My mother used to do it, but she had to give up driving because her sight's so poor, and there's no one else.'

At the farm Fiona made herself useful, loading earthy boxes of produce into the back of the van. She sniffed at a tub of basil and sighed, 'Oh, bliss,' and he said, 'The scent of the sun, don't you think?' He made her smell the dill too, which, he said, was the scent of the sea. She looked so excited and eager; it reawakened some of the same enthusiasm in himself.

Driving back she asked him what hours he worked, how much holiday he got.

'I start about six thirty,' he told her. 'Office work, while the place is quiet. And I finish about nine, ten in the evening. When dinner's over. There are slack moments during the day, obviously, but I have to be in the hotel. Around.'

'Every day?'

'In the season, yes. We're quieter other times. We close down altogether for a month after New Year.'

'It doesn't sound as if you have much time for a social life.'

'A manager for a chain hotel would have more free time.'

'You don't mind?'

'I have the guests. It's a sociable job. You have to like meeting people.'

'Even so. What about friends?'

'I count some of the guests as friends.'

'But they go away.'

'And come back. Some of them. You make what you can of things.' He smiled apologetically at her. 'I haven't put you off?'

'No, no.' She shook her head vehemently. 'I just, well, you must really love your job.'

He said, 'Yes, of course,' and thought: I did, once. He had just told her what he rarely told himself: that he had no time to himself, no real friendships. His job was his life. But he loved life, didn't he? So perhaps he still loved his job. He said, 'Yes,' again, more emphatically, but couldn't stop adding, because it was true too, 'My mother couldn't manage without me, in any case.'

Back at the hotel they unloaded the van at the kitchen entrance, where the boxes were received by Mrs Naughton, the daily help, who was an elderly, slow worker, but experienced and versatile, and without whose presence William would have felt unable to leave his mother.

'I've opened the bar,' Mrs Naughton announced. 'Two ladies wanted a bottle of wine. They're on the terrace.'

William nodded. He could guess which ladies.

'And,' Mrs Naughton went on, 'there's another guest, an older lady, looking for you. Says she's lost something. Sorry, didn't catch her name.'

'Right.' William showed Fiona the staff washbasin and while she was cleaning earth from her hands he poked his head into the snug bar, the lounge and the dining room. All were deserted. Perhaps whatever had been lost was now found.

Next he took ·Fiona up to the first floor and together they inspected three empty rooms allocated to two bookings due to arrive that afternoon. He ran his hands over surfaces, checked bathrooms, opened windows behind vases of fresh honeysuckle.

'In a big hotel there'd be a floor manager,' he told her. 'Responsible for all the rooms on a particular floor. Here, well, we're small. Most guests come for several nights. The cleaners pop in daily but I wouldn't until they left. Make sure they haven't forgotten anything. And then again before new guests arrive.'

Downstairs a telephone rang and, a second later, the reception bell clanged.

'Which first?' he asked Fiona, leading her quickly downstairs.

'The telephone?' Fiona suggested.

'Both at the same time, if I can manage it.' He swept into reception, said, 'Excuse me a moment,' to Katherine Jennings, who was dressed only in bikini and sarong and leaning against the counter. He picked up the telephone, listened to someone hesitantly making a dinner reservation for five for the weekend, and at the same time raised his eyebrows at Katherine. She mimed swigging from a glass. He smiled and, covering the telephone mouthpiece, murmured, 'Be with you right away.' Katherine raised a thumb, gave Fiona a broad grin, and marched back to the snug.

William finished on the telephone, wrote the booking down, and said, 'My mother or Mrs Naughton would have taken it eventually. There's an extension outside the kitchen.'

He led Fiona through to the snug where Katherine was perched on one of the bar stools, tapping a beer mat against the beaten copper bar.

'Ah,' she said, dropping the mat. 'Could we have another bottle of wine? Dry. White. Cold.' She smiled. 'Please.'

'I'll bring it out.' William turned to the chill cabinet.

'Great.' Katherine grinned again at Fiona, slipped off the stool, and left the room.

William took the bottle out alone. The women were sprawled on loungers, a low table between them, the previous empty bottle on the ground nearby. He placed two fresh glasses on the table and poured a measure of wine into each. Then stood the bottle between them.

'So,' said the woman Geraldine, who was lying on her front, wearing shorts and a loose, sleeveless top. Her lifted face was little more than a teasing grin and huge dark glasses. 'What's she got that we haven't?'

William smiled back at her. They were both tipsy, of course. 'Fiona Clayton is studying hotel management. She's shadowing me.'

'Ah,' said Geraldine. 'That's what they call it now, is it?' Both women laughed.

William picked up the dead glasses and empty bottle and turned to go.

'No.' Geraldine's lips puckered to a pout. 'Stay and chat for a while. You're always rushing off.'

'Of course,' said William. 'I'll be glad to. Just let me take these inside.'

Back in the snug he suggested Fiona have her lunch and, if she wanted to continue their arrangement, to come and find him again about three, in the office, when he'd show her the accounts computer and introduce her to hotel paperwork. He poured himself a mineral water and went back out.

The women had placed a garden chair between them, the far side of the low table. Geraldine was still on her stomach, her head nearest him, while Katherine had lifted her backrest and discarded her sarong to sun her front. Her legs were crossed at the ankle, her painted toenails almost touching his chair cushion. He pulled the chair away to sit down, lifted his glass, and said, 'Cheers, ladies.'

Both women echoed his toast. Katherine pressed her head back against the fabric of the chair and sighed, 'This place is magical. Beautiful building. Beautiful food.'

'Beautiful views,' murmured Geraldine, as if it was another echo, but fixing William with her dark glasses and lifting her front on to her elbows. The thin material of her top fell in a loose arc below her body, revealing a hanging pair of small white breasts. The nipples just brushed the inside of the material. Since William guessed he had been placed here intentionally, precisely to receive this view, he didn't remove his eyes. The curve of Geraldine's mouth approved his lack of embarrassment.

Katherine said, 'Geraldine doesn't believe you're the manager. Won't listen to me.'

Geraldine grinned at him. 'She's joking, isn't she?'

'Certainly not,' said William.

'William and his mother run the hotel together. I told you.'

'Your mother?' Geraldine looked baffled. 'Have I seen her?'

'The cook,' said Katherine, smug with knowledge. 'With the glasses. She's rather short-sighted, isn't she?'

'Something like that,' William agreed.

Geraldine regarded him with affront. 'The boss, already . . .'

'And she wants to know if there are any more like you hidden around here. I told her no, and that you're on the go from dawn till dusk. She's a deeply disappointed woman.'

'I'm sorry to hear that.'

Geraldine sighed. 'So no chance of your company this afternoon?'

'I'm afraid not. Perhaps this evening, after dinner . . .?'

'Well, perhaps.' The breasts jiggled with amusement. William's senses hovered between arousal and irritation. If this was still just flirting, it was faintly cruel. His role as manager gave him privileged access to the guests, but could also trap him, place him at their mercy. Katherine's presence suggested that this was still just a game, and he didn't enjoy the sensation of being played with.

A slim middle-aged woman in a safari-style cream dress and canvas lace-ups stepped out of the building on to the terrace, not four yards away. As her eyes fell on them she became immediately confused. Even took a step backwards, as if she had changed her mind about coming outside.

William rose instantly to greet her. 'Miss Henshaw. Can I get you anything? A lounger . . .?'

'No no.' Miss Henshaw overcame her confusion to smile at him. He smiled back and waited. Miss Henshaw had been coming to the hotel for years; he knew he had to be patient. As usual he was rewarded with a calm, much more organized response. 'I seem to have lost my binoculars. Stupid of me. I have a horrid feeling I left them downstairs last night. Possibly in the lounge. Perhaps someone has found them . . . one of the cleaners?'

'I'll check now.' This must be the loss Mrs Naughton had mentioned. William turned back to Katherine and Geraldine and said, 'If you'll excuse me . . .' Geraldine sighed extravagantly. Katherine rolled her eyes. He steered Miss Henshaw back into the building. 'Do you remember exactly . . .?'

'I was sitting near the window,' said Miss Henshaw. 'I lent them to a little boy to look at a sailing boat. I remember him giving them back, definitely. But . . .' She shrugged. 'After that . . . I can't remember.'

'We'll find them,' said William. 'Don't worry.'

Together they searched the lounge, but without success. William sent Miss Henshaw off to have her lunch and questioned the two cleaners, who were adamant that they had seen nothing. He checked with Mrs Naughton, and even his mother. He tactfully asked the few guests he came across if they had noticed the glasses, but no one had. This was bad news. Miss Henshaw was a keen birdwatcher – the fulmars and peregrines along the coast were what drew her here – and the binoculars essential to her hobby. They were also extremely expensive, quality glasses. And large, too. Not something that could be accidentally dropped into the wrong bag without the recipient noticing. The tediousness and disruption of lost valuables bore down on him. As a last resort the hotel would refund Miss Henshaw their cost and claim it on their own insurance, but this would not help Miss Henshaw now, and nor was a reputation for lax security good for business. Miss Henshaw's modest refusal to make a fuss about it, when, at two thirty, he found her and apologized for his lack of progress, only made him more frustrated. He lent her a pair of his own binoculars from the office but knew that they were inferior to her own, and an inadequate substitute. And, as if he didn't have enough to put up with, the women on the terrace were being exasperating. They had requested lunch outside and every time he passed within earshot – which was quite often – they made loud, patronizing remarks to each other. 'Still busy, poor boy.' 'A manager's job is never done.' 'Legalized slavery, I'd call it.' There was a lack of respect in their voices that was quite insufferable; though suffer it he had to, since sharpness to a guest was unthinkable.

At three he realized that he had overlooked his own lunch and made himself a sandwich in the kitchen. He was interrupted twice by phone calls and, while taking the second call at reception, spotted Fiona in the office behind. He had quite forgotten about their arrangement. He apologized profusely, blaming the distraction of Miss Henshaw's loss, and suggested they try another session tomorrow, as he was now quite behind in his duties. Fiona agreed with such alacrity and understanding that he regretted her absence the moment she was gone. She's what I need, he thought. A girl like her. An assistant. Even a boy. Company. Help. For days like this. Except the hotel couldn't possibly afford it. His father, of course, had had himself.

At four the first of the new arrivals turned up, followed within half an hour by the second. These were a couple with a disabled child, for whom various special arrangements had to be made. Soon afterwards guests who had been out for the day trickled back; when he could, between other duties, he caught them and mentioned the missing binoculars, but nobody remembered seeing them. Tomorrow, he knew, he would have to report the loss to the police. Not that they would send anyone out – and he certainly wouldn't encourage a visit – but simply to obtain a crime number for the insurance company. Miss Henshaw had had a wasted day, and would indeed have a wasted holiday, if they remained unfound.

The barman, Joe, turned up at six with his sister-in-law, who was the evening waitress. Both had been working the previous night but both also claimed not to have seen the glasses. William believed them, as he had the cleaners earlier. All had worked at the hotel for at least six weeks, during which time nothing of value had inexplicably disappeared. Employee thieves never waited long before they struck. He went up to his own room to shower and change and under the water spray indulged himself in two common fantasies: first, that some cataclysm would happen that would force his mother to give up work, or at least bring home to her the impossibility of their situation, prompting her to gracefully retire; and second, because the first caused him such pain – his mother was passionate about her work, she would be bereft – that he would meet and marry a woman as entranced with hotel life as he had once been, a woman with inexhaustible energy and patience, who would love and protect his mother as fiercely as he did, and whose beautiful, willing body would await him, nightly, in this very room. It occurred to him, drying himself, and knowing that his mother's failing eyesight would one day force the issue, that only the second was a true fantasy.

There were nine tables occupied for dinner – almost a full house. William deliberately allocated Katherine and Geraldine's side of the room to the waitress so he wouldn't have to serve them. On another occasion he might have been entertained by their banter, but not tonight. The hotel served dinner only between seven and eight – no non-resident meals on weekdays – so by nine he could leave the waitress to cope and went into the kitchen to have his own dinner with his mother. The steel surfaces were already spotless and the dishwashers loaded, though because the machines were old and noisy they wouldn't be turned on until the dining room was empty. After dinner he washed up their plates by hand and then accompanied his mother to her room. He stayed chatting for twenty minutes, during which time he checked that she had everything she needed to hand and read her details of radio programmes from the listings magazine. He left her with a pot of jasmine tea and the radio on.

In the dining room the waitress was busy laying tables for breakfast and in the snug Joe was serving drinks and coffee. William sought out Miss Henshaw, who was reading in the lounge, sat down beside her, and confessed that he hadn't found her binoculars.

'Well,' said Miss Henshaw, 'that'll teach me to be more careful, won't it.' She smiled at him bravely. 'Silly me.'

'No,' said William. He tried to explain that losses in the building were the hotel's responsibility, not the residents', but she just shook her head. He recommended they report the loss to the police, for insurance purposes, but she insisted no fuss or action was taken at all. He was sure she was being kind to him personally, because she had known him since he was a boy, and somehow this kindness was difficult to bear.

'Claiming for them is simple,' he pressed. 'Just a few forms. Please let me do it.'

'No,' she said. 'You have enough on your plate already. I don't want to add to it.' If she had been a less inhibited person, William thought, she would have patted him on the hand. He felt depressed. A good hotelier made the work seem light, easy, nothing at all. A good hotelier didn't have concessions – ridiculous, expensive concessions – made for them by sympathetic guests. He said, 'You're too kind, Miss Henshaw,' and sighed goodnight to her.

In the corridor outside he was caught by Mr and Mrs Clayton.

'Fiona's told us all about this morning,' Mrs Clayton said warmly. 'We would have thanked you at dinner, but you were so busy . . .'

William wondered where Fiona was. He would have welcomed a chat, an injection of her enthusiasm.

'She's upstairs already,' Mrs Clayton went on, 'or she'd have thanked you herself. Some television programme she never misses.' She chuckled indulgently.

'Do tell her my offer for tomorrow stands,' said William, hoping he sounded sincere, not just formally polite. Sometimes even he found it hard to tell the difference. 'As early as she likes. I enjoyed her company.'

'Oh, we will,' Mrs Clayton trilled. 'Of course we will.'

In the bar he helped himself to an ice lager, the first alcoholic drink of the day. 'Take your weight off,' Joe murmured, and William nodded at him – he was a good barman, Joe, never asked for help – and said, 'I intend to.'

As he settled himself on a stool the customer side of the bar someone tapped him on the shoulder.

'Free now?' It was Geraldine suddenly beside him, looking very black-eyed and sultry.

'Absolutely.' He swivelled to face her. She drew up another bar stool and sat down.

'My sister's gone to bed.' She chuckled. 'Crashing headache. Out of practice, these married women. No stamina.'

Geraldine, William thought, looked as if she had plenty of stamina. Fit like an athlete. He guessed, wearily, that he would probably spend the rest of the evening with her. And if she suggested more? He didn't know. Maybe. It would be a kind of recompense. And self-denial took energy.

Joe closed the bar at eleven, and by then William and Geraldine were the only customers left. Geraldine had become increasingly friendly. She had touched him several times in the last hour, light brushes on the arm, the shoulder, most recently on the thigh. The waitress helped her brother-in-law clean up and restock the bottles for the next day, and when they'd finished William followed them to the staff entrance door and locked it behind them. Geraldine was waiting for him in the hallway behind. He turned to see her laughing silently into the back of her strong tanned wrist.

'What's so funny?' He had had three lagers himself now; he felt relaxed, loosened up. Whatever the joke, he was prepared to share it.

'How about some room service?' She could hardly contain her mirth. 'Sorry. Just struck me as funny . . .'

He laughed. It wasn't an original invitation, but at least it was clear. He felt himself slide easily over the guest/ management divide, and, coming to stand close to her, murmured, 'It'd be a pleasure.'

Following her upstairs he reminded himself that liking these women wasn't necessary. That the liaisons actually worked better with the emotions unengaged. He would be following with much more ambivalence, much more intimation of loss, if the body in front of his was, say, Fiona's. This woman was like himself, concerned only with physical pleasure. And she was physically pleasing. Indeed her bottom, swaying tautly in front of him, a just-discernible pantie-line bisecting each buttock, was quite mesmerizing.

Inside her room she closed the door behind them. As the catch clicked in its socket William felt the last weight of the day drop from him. He was now off duty. In here, shut away from the rest of the hotel, they were just man and woman. About to do what men and women did.

He caught her hips, drew her close, and kissed her. Like drinking a rare, robust, fierce-flavoured wine. Even her lips were muscular.

She pulled back, licked at the corners of her mouth, and started to unbutton his shirt. 'So, Mr Manager. Do you do this often?'

'Certainly not. Do you?'

She laughed throatily. 'Depends what you mean by often.' When his shirt was fully undone she crossed her arms at her waist and pulled off her silky top. A lace-trimmed quarter-bra pushed her breasts upwards into impossibly firm half-spheres. Adventurers, in William's experience, always wore exotic underwear, or none at all. She undid a clip at the front and discarded the bra. Her eyes mocked his expression. She whispered, 'What would your mother say?'

'That she trusted my discretion. She's not a prude.' Necessary lies. His mother would be shocked, probably. But then blame herself, feeling her demands, or those of the job, had driven him to it.

Geraldine pushed the flats of her hands under his shirt, across his chest. She regarded his flesh meditatively. 'Mmm. Just as nice close up.'

He didn't understand. Her lips twitched. 'Were you aware of being watched? This morning. On the beach?'

He grasped what she meant, and automatically glanced across to the window. 'No,' he said, astonished. 'I wasn't.'

She was still stroking him. On the window sill was a pair of binoculars. He found her wrists and stilled her hands. Large, expensive-looking binoculars.

'Hey,' she said, pulling against his grip.

'Are those yours?'

She looked across the room, saw what he was looking at. 'Whoops.' She bit her lip, her eyelashes batting. 'Caught red-handed.'

He could think of nothing adequate to say. Here he was, in the room of a half-naked, willing woman, actually holding her, and there were the binoculars. He had been looking for them for hours. She knew he had. She thought the discovery funny. He pushed her aside and walked over to the window.

'These are Miss Henshaw's,' he said.

Geraldine came up behind him. Carelessly she said, 'She left them in the lounge last night. Kathy told me about your morning strolls. I was going to take them down tomorrow.'

'Why didn't you return them today?'

She laughed. 'What? Admit I'd taken them? And why. Ha!'

'You could have said you'd found them. Or left them somewhere obvious.'

'Well I didn't.' She pulled at him impatiently. 'Come on. You should feel flattered. They're only a stupid pair of binoculars.'

He resisted. 'Miss Henshaw uses them for birdwatching. They are very important to her.'

'For goodness sake.' Geraldine was scornful. 'Silly old bat. Do her good to do something different.'

William could feel rage rising in him. 'You have stolen from one of my guests.'

'Borrowed, not stolen. Your guests.' She said the words with a sneer. 'Don't be so pompous. Honestly.'

He felt like striking her. Slapping her naked flesh. Her body was beautiful, callous, totally self-centred. He had been about to have sex with her. His own body still wanted to but to do it, now, would be an act of utter betrayal. He started to rebutton his shirt.

'What the hell d'you think you're doing?' Geraldine tried to push his hands away.

Firmly he persisted. 'I'm taking these downstairs, now.'

'I thought,' she said acidly, 'that the guest was always right.'

'Not always.' His shirt was done up. He picked up the binoculars.

She looked at him with hard eyes. 'You are a pompous little prig.' She tried to touch his genitals but he turned his body away. 'Well, fuck you.'

'Cover yourself up,' he said.

'Oh.' She put her hands on her hips and swung her breasts at him. 'So now I offend you, do I? God, you hypocrite, Mr Holier than Thou. Panting for it a moment ago.'

'You have stolen from and insulted another guest. It's unforgivable.' He knew he did sound pompous. He couldn't help it. He was saying what he felt.

She was suddenly savage. 'What a sad little life you must lead,' she hissed. 'Sad little boy, playing the sad little manager in your sad little hotel, getting your sad little screws where you can. You and your fucking mother. What a life. Pathetic.'

'I would like you to leave in the morning.' William kept his voice steady. 'With or without your sister.' He had never before asked a guest to leave, though he remembered his father doing so once, also for blatant theft. He was perfectly within his rights. He had even thought of saying it before she said 'fucking mother'.

'You've got a nerve.' Her mouth was twisted with outrage. 'And what if I tell everybody—'

'Say what you like.' He lifted the binoculars to where she could see them clearly. 'But you'll only look a fool.' It was the closest he had ever come to insulting a guest, and it made him feel hot. He moved to the door. 'I will say nothing to anyone about where I found these or why you are leaving, but I would like you to go straight after breakfast. Certainly before ten.'

He didn't wait to receive more abuse; he could see she was boiling with it. He closed the door and walked quickly down the dim-lit stairs to the office, where he locked the binoculars in the safe. His hands, turning the dial, were shaking.

Up in his own room he lay back on his bed and waited for his mind to stop racing. He was experiencing a powerful sense of alarm. But it wasn't rational. Geraldine wouldn't say anything to anyone, except perhaps her sister; she had too much to lose herself. Even the fact that he had been in her room, if his motive were exposed, would reflect more odium on her than him. It was obvious to everyone what sort of woman she was. She had to be ten years his senior. She, not he, would be seen as the exploiter. Besides which, practically nothing of a sexual nature, in the end, had happened.

He resolved, however, to give her a wide berth in the morning. A woman like her might be impulsive, spiteful. Irrational. She might accept damage to herself as a worthwhile price for damaging him. His very presence might be provocative. As long as she did as she was told, and left before ten, he would take pains to leave her alone. That would be the humane thing to do, in any case.

He slept eventually, and woke as usual just before six. After taking his mother a cup of tea, and having one himself, he went to the office and made out a bill for both Geraldine and Katherine, keeping the accounts separate in case Katherine decided to stay on alone. He thought this unlikely, however, since they had arrived in the same car. He put the bills in envelopes, wrote their names on the outside, and placed the envelopes on their table in the dining room. Then returned to the office and concentrated on paperwork.

At the back of his mind, as the hour passed, he heard the hotel slowly come alive. Noises above, doors opening and closing. Pipes hissing. A faint, just detectable smell of grilled bacon, coffee. A domestic clatter somewhere closer. At quarter to eight he rose. Breakfast would now be on the sideboard, or in the process of being carried there. Time for his walk.

Outside the office he hesitated. Further down the corridor, almost outside the dining room, one of the walk-in cupboard doors was ajar. The cleaners' cupboard. Odd. He walked quickly up to it – no human sounds from the dining room yet – and glanced inside. One of the vacuum cleaners was open and empty, presumably awaiting a new dirt bag, but otherwise everything looked as it should. He closed the door firmly and, avoiding the open dining-room door, left the building.

But the walk along the beach, usually reviving, was an effort today. The sense of being alone, separate from the hotel, had been spoilt for him. Geraldine had spoilt it. Today he felt no inclination to remove his shirt; it would be a self-conscious, embarrassing, not liberating act. He was tired. Tired of the hotel. Tired of the guests. Tired of the responsibility. He wished his father hadn't died. He wished he hadn't said yes, with such naive, unthinking eagerness, at the age of twenty, when his mother suggested he take his father's place. He wished his mother's sight was perfect, so she could employ anyone, or that she was helplessly blind, so that, even if he still had to care for her, it need not be here. Either way, he would regain an element of choice. He was a young man, but he felt middle aged. He wanted his youth back.

Somewhere behind him, up at the hotel, a car engine started up. Early for someone to be leaving. He hoped it was Geraldine and her sister. Whoever it was, they were driving fast, racing through the gears. He listened to the sound rise and fade, heading towards town. He bet it was them, roaring away from trouble. He hoped they hadn't stripped their rooms of towels, ashtrays, vases. Petty acts of revenge. He hoped they had left a cheque somewhere for him. But the hopes were mere thoughts, no emotion behind them. As long as they were gone.

And now there was someone on the terrace. Someone waving at him. Running towards him. A small, young, flying figure. Fiona. Something was wrong. He strode towards her, thinking immediately, heartstoppingly, of his mother.

'William,' she gasped, running up to him. She turned and tugged at his arm, urging him back to the hotel. 'Come quickly. Quickly!' She was close to tears. In her free hand she was flapping something, an envelope. She thrust it distractedly at him. 'It's from those women. I'd come down early, because you told my parents I could, and they met me just as I was going in to breakfast. They said to give it to you. William, I think they've done something terrible.'

William tore open the envelope as he jogged up the steps to the terrace. Inside was a cheque, and a folded paper napkin. On the napkin was written: 'Hope everyone enjoys breakfast!!!' He slowed, staring at it.

'Come on!' moaned Fiona. 'Other people will be down soon. I put oven cloths over them, but . . .'

He followed her through the French windows of the lounge, along the corridor to the dining room.

'Thank god, thank god,' Fiona said. 'No one here yet. Look. Look.' She whipped cloths off the three dishes on the sideboard, and lifted one of the lids. William knew what he was going to see. Under a mass of filth – dust, grit, hairs, fluff, all the detritus a vacuum cleaner bag contained – were what had once been grilled plum tomatoes, the black gills of field mushrooms.

'It's in all three.' Fiona was anguished. She picked up another lid. Somewhere under the filth should be scrambled eggs. There was actually an alive, maimed moth, fluttering amongst the mess. 'Horrible, horrible.'

William said quietly. 'Does my mother know?'

Fiona shook her head quickly, as if it was a straw to cling to. 'I don't think so. Really, I don't think so. She actually came in with toast, while the lids were off . . . but I don't think she could see them . . .'

'No,' said William. A leaden weight had settled in his guts. This was the cataclysm. It had to be. He could stop other guests seeing the revolting messes, but new breakfasts would have to be cooked. An explanation given to his mother. Even if he did the cooking himself, he couldn't do it secretly. She was there, in the kitchen. She would have to be told. She would know that only extraordinary luck had prevented a disaster. She would be devastated.

Fiona was peering at him, reading him. 'Tell her there's been an accident,' she urged. 'Tell her . . . tell her . . .' She lifted up the lid of the china coffee jug and said, 'Ugh,' clamping it down again. Then glanced around to the side table, with its boxes of cereal and jugs of juice. 'They're all right,' she said. 'It's just over here. Tell her . . .' She lifted all three lids from the dishes and feverishly started to pour what had once been coffee, now thick with dirt and hairs, over the contents. When it was empty she folded the jug into one of the cloths, and banged the bundle violently against the wall. There was a dull clatter of breaking china. She opened the cloth and scattered the shards over the swimming mess in the dishes. 'Tell her I did it. That I'm terribly, terribly sorry. That I was just holding the jug, and I dropped it, and there's mess everywhere. Oh God. Oh God.' She put a hand to her mouth and, as if she really had done it, and was indeed most terribly, terribly sorry, burst into tears.

He put a gentle hand on her back. Patted her. Acknowledged to himself that it would work. He would simply take the dishes and jugs back to the kitchen, slide all the messes into the bin, tell his mother that there had been a ridiculous accident and how upset Fiona was, and his mother would rush out to comfort and reassure the girl, believe her tears – who wouldn't, when they were genuine? – while he washed the dishes; and in ten minutes or so new breakfasts would be on the side. The leaden weight had gone. But so had the window above. The window he had dreamed of. The moment when his mother might have asked *can we go on?* And when he might have found the courage to confess *I'm not sure I want to.* What Geraldine's wickedness had handed him, had been snatched away again by Fiona's generosity. And because the option had been given him, and because the cataclysm was, to some degree, his own fault, he would have to take it.

He patted her again on the back, and then, with his hands wrapped in the oven cloths, picked up the first two dishes.

One day, he thought. But not this day.

ATOMS AND MOLECULES

In her hand Laura carried a dead moth, taken from the sitting room window sill. A moth that was just atoms and molecules now, because its life was ended, and which was about to become a flower.

Carefully she planted her feet on the biggest stone at the edge of the small garden pond, squatted down so low her bare knees brushed her cheeks, and flipped the dead moth on to the water surface.

Here they were, instantly: the flower-makers. She held her breath. From the dark black-plastic edges of the pond, their weight not even denting the water surface, as the weight of their parents did, shot the baby skaters. Dozens of them, so minuscule, fast, and hungry. Within ten seconds the moth was no longer visible, and the angled bodies of the pondskaters, their jaws clamped into it, drinking its flesh, had created the flower. Found their place on the corpse, their special, ordered place, and formed a floating, spiky, pale brown thistle-head.

Like magic.

On the rock behind was a wolf spider. There were three that lived around the pond. They were made of atoms and molecules too. Wolf spiders were small, compared to house spiders, more muscular and compact. They didn't weave

webs. Wolf spiders hunted, stalked, and ambushed. Sometimes they appeared to be sunning themselves on the bare
stones. Laura worried about the wolf spiders when grown-
ups came close, because grown-ups didn't seem to notice
them like she did. But luckily the spiders could see them,
or their shadows, or perhaps feel the tremble of the earth,
and zipped into cover as they approached. And she didn't
worry about how the wolf spiders would manage next
year when the pond was gone, because she'd seen them on
rocks in other parts of the garden and knew they didn't
need water.

Somewhere under the marsh marigold leaves would be
the frog. Lots of atoms and molecules there. The frog sat
under the leaves with just her nose out of the water, for
hours, sometimes. Laura's father had taken all her babies
away. He had scooped out the spawn and taken it down to
the canal, because he said there was too much for the
pond, that the tadpoles would use all the oxygen, and that
the last remaining goldfish would suffocate. Laura hadn't
objected. The idea that all that jelly, buckets of it, had come
out of one frog; well, that was magic too. But a rather
disgusting magic. Last year they had let the frogspawn
hatch and the pond had seethed with wriggling bodies
that looked like shiny black slime if you caught them in a
net, and two of the fish had died. So this year the pretty
frog was on her own, childless.

A wasp came down to drink the pondwater, landing
on some just-submerged weed. Half the thistle-head
disintegrated and rushed off to investigate. The wasp
wriggled, showing the baby skaters it was alive, and they
lost interest, scooting back to the moth carcass again.

Somewhere at the bottom of the pond would be the
monsters that turned into dragonflies. Atoms and molecules
that made the ugliest, most ferocious-looking insects in the

garden. Even uglier than cockchafers, more ferocious than Devil's Coach Horse beetles. They ate tadpoles, and they didn't need as much oxygen as fish, so they'd been in seventh heaven last year. But Laura's father had said that they wouldn't starve without the tadpoles. Plenty of other pondlife for them to eat.

Time was running out for Laura to catch one of the monsters turning into a dragonfly. They climbed up the water irises and slipped out of their dragon suits so neatly you thought they were still there, till you looked closely. She had taken two of their empty shells to school to show the teacher, and everyone gasped. More than five centimetres long. But, even so, the beautiful dragonfly must have been doubled up inside. They were brilliant, iridescent blue creatures, zooming and whirring over the water like felt-pen-sized helicopters, the largest insects in the garden.

Perhaps she'd ask her father to look out for monsters crawling up the irises when he did his gardening in the evening. You could ask him to do anything these days and he'd say yes. He had a look on his face as if he was dreaming about something delicious, like ice-cream, and even when he had to tell you something sad, like the pond would have to be filled in, he didn't look sad. He tried, but his smile was still there, just under his lips. He'd said he'd buy an indoor tank for the goldfish, if it was still alive, and they'd take the frog somewhere where there were other frogs, so she wouldn't be so lonely. Laura had warned him that frogs often went back to places they knew, so it must be a pond a long way away, otherwise she might try to make the journey only to find her old home gone.

The baby was the reason for her father being so helpful. It would be born in September, and it just being there in her mother's stomach was a miracle. Like she, nine years ago, had been the first miracle. That was what her parents had said. They'd told her they'd waited years for her and when she finally came they thought she would be the only one. They'd dug the pond for her when she was six, because everyone said there wouldn't be another. But now it had happened, and they were sorry but ponds were dangerous for little children, so it would have to go.

She had listened to the baby's heartbeat in her mother's stomach – it was much faster than her own. She had felt the baby kick against her hand. She'd even seen it, sort of, on a screen in the hospital. They couldn't tell whether it was a baby boy or girl because it was facing the wrong way, so they couldn't see if it had a penis or not. But it had a big nodding head and you could see its chest pulsing through its back. She was looking forward to seeing the new baby properly and being able to hold it and learn all about it; it was just a shame that so many animals would have to die, because of her or him. She had persuaded her father to leave filling in the pond till the winter – her mother said the baby wouldn't even be crawling by then – and made him promise that he wouldn't do it without her being there, so that she could rescue anything that needed rescuing. What happened to the pond skaters in the winter? And there would be water snails, and the whirligig beetles.

But what her school teacher had told her about atoms and molecules was stopping her feeling too sad. Her teacher had said that everything in the world was made of atoms, which were tiny particles, much smaller even than grains of sand, and when they joined together with other atoms they were called molecules. She said that the atoms and molecules in living things weren't very different from each other. It didn't matter what the animal was, the same atoms and molecules would be there. And that they didn't die or disappear when an animal died, they just joined up in a different way and became something else.

So it was possible that the atoms and molecules in her parents' baby had once lived in a pond like this. The baby was floating in water now, her mother said, so it wouldn't even be that strange for them. And when the pond was filled in, the atoms and molecules that made up the tiny creatures living there might, one day, end up in another baby. Or in another animal that lived in a pond. A tadpole, maybe, or a ferocious dragonfly larva. Or a flower. Laura had seen how this could happen, because of watching the baby skaters and the dead moth. So even though lots of animals had to die for her parents' baby, it wasn't the end for them. Nothing ended. Atoms and molecules went on forever.

DELIVERY

A decade or more back, Harry had seen off Social Services with his axe. The two women had called at the cottage, ignored all his shouts to go away, and had left only when, finally, he snatched open the front door – with the axe in his hand. Not lifted threateningly; merely hanging, head down, from his slack right arm. But it had done the trick; they left, and never returned.

Harry kept the axe in the hallway after that, when it was not in use. Though uses were frequent; axes were versatile tools. With it he smashed up the wooden pallets that his next door neighbour left outside his gate, shattering the soft wood to kindling, which, when the evenings became dark and cold, he burnt in his small grate. (His nephew said he should thank the neighbour for his generosity. Why? Harry thought. The man owned a builder's yard down in the village, the pallets cost him nothing; he was merely disposing of them for free.)

He also used the axe as a hammer. Harry often nailed things. The nails came free with the pallets, either bursting from the grain as he smashed them up, or collecting in the bottom of the firegrate after the wood had burnt away. He used the nails, and strips of wood from the pallets, to board up the back door. Tapped the heads in with the flat side of the axe head. How could you guard two doors, at opposite sides of the house? And all that draught.

Once – Harry admitted he had been feeling very distant that day, very locked in the past – he had nailed his own hand to the kitchen table. He had solved the problem of holding the nail upright, ready for the blow, by laying his hand on the surface palm upwards, and steadying the nail in curled-over fingers. The funny thing was that, at the same time as he was lining up the impaling stroke, he had been frightened of missing, and directly striking his flesh. But his aim had been true. The nail embedded itself deeply enough to make a spike under the wooden table top. There had been very little blood. Only a brief shock of pain. The briefness had disconcerted him. However, for the half day he sat immobilised on the kitchen chair – before releasing himself with an underarm, under-table swing of the axe – he had felt temporarily relieved. Temporarily restored. Once freed, he had worked the nail from his flesh under the ice-cold winter tap water, and his hand now bore only the tiniest of scars.

Today, when rapping on the front door summoned him, the axe was in its usual place, propped below the row of wall nails that acted as coat pegs. But today Harry opened the door without checking first, because it was a Sunday – he had heard the village church bells not an hour ago – and knew it would be his nephew, Joe, with the groceries. He swung the door open and moved forward to block the threshold with his body, as he always did. Even Joe couldn't be relied on not to try to carry the box inside.

'Here you are then, Harry,' Joe grinned at him, a foolish, ingratiating grin. His nephew, Harry thought, had been an ugly pug of a young man, and now, in middle age, was a physical disgrace. Did some soft factory job that had left cushions of idleness around his waist. At his age, Harry had been hard as a nut. Strong as the steel he worked with.

'And,' said Joe, stepping to one side, revealing another figure behind the box he was holding, 'this is my boy, Neil. Now Harry—'

Harry grasped the box, interrupting him. He tried to back into the hall.

'No,' said Joe, still smiling, but firmly now. He put a steadying hand on the open door. 'You listen a minute, Harry. You remember what I told you last week?'

Over the top of the cardboard box Harry stared at the boy Neil. The panic subsided. He was a boy. As tall as his father, but slim as a whip. Blonde hair tucked behind his ears. Something glinted on an earlobe. An earring? Jewellery? But he was, undoubtedly, a boy. His nephew's son. Since he had never seen him before, he had to take this on trust.

'D'you remember, Harry? I warned you last week. I'll be working Sundays up to Christmas now. Just brought Neil round so it doesn't surprise you, like. Next Sunday he'll bring the stuff. Got his driving test a month ago, clever lad. It'll be same as usual. Only him, not me. OK?'

'Hello, Mr Daniels.' The boy's eyelashes batted like a girl's. 'It'll be a pleasure.'

'He's your uncle,' Joe chided him. 'Not Mr Daniels. It's your great uncle Harry.'

Harry wanted to say something, but it was days since he had last spoken out loud and his throat muscles took a while to respond. Before he had made more than a creaking noise Joe tapped the box and said, 'Two dozen candles in there, in case you're low. You'll be needing them, now the hour's changed. Slow burners, guaranteed. You tell Neil, now, if there's anything special you want for next week.'

Harry shook his head. He didn't want anyone here instead of Joe. Certainly not that boy. He had a face that had escaped from somewhere.

He closed the door against Joe's feet and carried the box

into the living room. After a minute he heard car doors slam, an engine fire and fade. They had gone.

His mind thudded. Was it a trick? After all these years, were they trying to catch him out? His hands shook, unpacking the box. As usual he tossed the apples to one side. What use were apples to a man? The boy's face flashed vivid in his mind. Just like Lizzie. Had they known? Waited all these years, knowing the boy would one day look right, and then brought him to the cottage, trailed him like a lure. Had he reacted? Betrayed anything? He couldn't picture himself. Couldn't remember.

All afternoon and evening his thoughts raced. In the candlelight their destinations darkened; the corners of the room guttered with the most patient, devious revenges. Was this why her family had kept him alive, all these years? His own brothers had given up on him decades ago. What thanks had he ever given them? What did they get out of it? How innocent, how stupid of him. He had never considered motives.

Late evening he heated up a can of Chunky Vegetable soup on his camping stove and spooned it down with half a packet of digestive biscuits. He had been cold earlier, he realized. But afterwards, though he was less chilled, he still felt threatened enough to nail up the front door. Just with a pallet plank, and six warped, charcoal-blackened nails. It was the act of doing it, really. It wouldn't take a moment to prise off next time he wanted to go outside.

All week, as he pottered through the dark, mildew-stained rooms, he dreamed. The dreams lurched to and fro in time. Snippets of his past. He remembered how, even at the beginning, just after Lizzie's death, her family had rallied to him. How their men had stood, stiff and protective, around him at the funeral. No, you'd expect that, wouldn't you? Not strange at all. She was one of them. Of course they'd grieved for her too. Joe had been a child then, no more than ten or twelve, puffed up and red-faced, because he was black-suited with the men, not behind curtains with the women.

And perhaps in the five years afterwards, while he was still working, contact would have been natural. Joe's father, her brother, God rest his soul, had been a crane driver at the steel works. Of course they exchanged words, nods. Nothing suspicious in that.

But afterwards? When he stopped going to work? When the retreat he hadn't realized possible, until any alternative became impossible, came suddenly upon him? As if a cloak of numbness had lifted, exposing a nakedness of raw, flinching, appalled flesh. Why, then, had they followed him here? Sought him out, tried to cajole him into the world again, and, when that failed, kept tabs on him, took over responsibility for his survival. They held his invalidity book. Now his pension book. Paid his bills, few as they were. Just water, these days, and some new property tax. Shopped for him, food and occasional clothes, brought boxes round weekly. Why? And why for so long? Even after her brother died, when there was no one left who could truly remember her, why?

Because he dozed frequently during the day, he was awake for long periods at night. When the grate had burnt to cold white ash and only the faint haze of the nightlight candle near the door relieved the blackness, his thoughts became more fantastic. He saw the family in a huddle, heads together, whispering. A cabal, planning, plotting. Thinking long-term. Perhaps the boy wasn't one of them at all, but some-one searched for over the years. An actor, specially chosen. Or – the limits dissolved in the dark – even manufactured. Blueprinted, put together, moulded by them, over many years, in her likeness.

In daylight his thoughts were easier to order, and of lesser scope. He wondered, at one point, if they simply wanted the cottage. Perhaps they thought that, by showing him the boy, they could scare him to death. Thought they'd earned his property. But they wouldn't get it. He had made no will; his own relatives, not hers, would inherit. And they must know this. Everyone understood inheritance.

So, if it was a confession they wanted from him, they would have to try harder. Shock couldn't do it. They would have to be more inventive, more cunning than that. He had seen through their plot.

By Sunday morning he had almost convinced himself that, when the door banged later, it would be Joe as usual behind it. That the boy had been a one-off, a tactic that, having failed, they wouldn't try again.

He heard the church bells, and padded expectantly round the house. After a while it came to him that Joe was late. Perhaps that was it . . . last week had been his final visit. He had brought the boy with him to show him why. After twenty five years of keeping him alive, they were now abandoning him. They had grown bored with their game.

Then the door rattled. Harry strode to the hall, slipped the blade of the axe under the plank of wood, frowning at it – had he really not been out for seven days? – and prised it off. He propped the axe against the wall again and opened the door.

'Sorry I'm a bit late, Mr Daniels.' The boy's head was tilted almost to his shoulder in apology. 'Hope you haven't been worrying. I was out last night. Headache like a pile-driver this morning.' He smiled radiantly down into the box he was holding. 'But it's all here.'

Harry didn't take the box off him immediately. He wanted another look at the boy's face, while he was trapped in front of him. Lizzie had been older, of course. But the same golden hair. The same pale, angelic complexion. The same incongruously dark, long eyelashes. Indecently long, on a boy. And the same radiant smile. But what had the boy said? Something about headaches. Aha, aha. He felt clever, to have spotted the reference. That clinched it. Aches and pains. Headaches, bellyaches. She must have told them, all those years ago. They must have passed it down, one generation to the next.

He found his arms reaching out for the box; which was a mistake, because it suddenly came to him that the boy should be inside the cottage. That inside was where he belonged. Where he had escaped from. Now it was too late. As he took the weight his throat grumbled but, without words in his head, he could form nothing aloud.

'D'you want anything special for next week, Mr Daniels? You only got to say. And Mam says do you need any more blankets, now it's getting colder?'

Harry started to shake his head, as he always did, but then caught himself. No. That was it. Load the boy up. It would provide an excuse. He nodded curtly.

'More blankets? Yes?' The boy's eyes urged him to confirm it.

'Hmm.' He nodded again, more emphatically.

The boy looked delighted. Proud he had forced a response.

'That's fine, Mr Daniels. I won't forget. See you next week then.' And he waved, actually waved, as he walked back to Joe's car.

Harry banged the door shut with his knee. As he thumped the box on to the cottage table he felt cross with himself. A missed opportunity. A whole week to wait. He unloaded the box and, throwing the apples aside, found himself transferring the anger. Headaches and bellyaches. Always headaches and bellyaches. Not in the early days, of course, when he'd taken her out on his arm, oh no. Then she had flashed like a beacon, batted those lashes, bestowed that radiance. Flattering, when they were courting. A woman, as young and beautiful as she; made him feel a prince. But afterwards, when she was a married woman, it hadn't been seemly. A seemly woman, a woman he could trust, he would have allowed her freedom. A seemly woman could have had friends, as many as she wished, could have come and gone as she pleased. But could she understand this? She could not. Instead of moderating her behaviour, she had sulked. Sulked and complained. Headaches and belly-aches. When he wanted to touch her. Or when she wanted to escape from him. Visiting the doctor. How could he say no to her seeing the doctor? Except that there was never anything wrong. Excuses, excuses. Visiting her mother, or a friend, more like; or strolling the town. He'd caught her in a lie several times. There were rights and duties in marriage. No one could say he hadn't been a good husband, no one: a mature man, with a steady, well-paid job, even a house of his own. He'd been tolerant, and self-controlled. Some men hit their misbehaving wives. Not he. Not once. Never. He had loved her. Even told her so – not kept it to himself, like so many husbands. But you had to be firm. Had to set boundaries. Force boundaries on them, if necessary.

A sense of outrage built in him overnight. He hardly slept. How dare, how dare, her family stir him up again like this. And as he pushed the anger on to them, he felt it slip from her. Dear Lizzie. She was as she was. She'd given him four years of joy, while they courted. More than a year of pride and contentment, when they were first married. Then two years of frustration and disappointment, and then her death. On balance, in shortened form, probably much like any other marriage. Ups and down, but the good outweighing the bad. All marriages ended in acrimony, or death.

The next day he went upstairs, the first time in many months. Across the stairwell spiders had slung dusty hammocks that stretched and collapsed to dirty string as he walked through them. He went into the bedroom where the double bedstead, unslept in for thirty years, still stood in the middle of the room. The bare mattress was velvety with dust. He opened the wardrobe and touched her dresses. Silly styles. He had loved the full, fussy, petticoated frocks the girls wore in his own youth; these that had followed were skimpy, shapeless things. Bold colours, bold designs, but not womanly. They had been hers, though, and she had still looked beautiful in them.

He removed his favourite, a blue sleeveless dress with white piping round the armholes and neck that she had thought dull, but he thought made her look like a blonde Jackie Kennedy. Or Princess Grace. All the posh women had them. He carried the dress downstairs on its hanger, hammered a nail into a beam near the window with the back of the axe, and hung the dress from it, so he could sit in front of the evening fire and still see it. It upset him, especially when it swayed as he brushed past, but it was a reminder. He didn't want the feelings to fade before next Sunday.

Over the days, he tidied up a little. If he was to have a visitor, and such a special visitor, he didn't want to give the impression of having lost his grip. He didn't want to be pitied. He could do nothing about the mildew on the walls, the stains on the carpet around the camping stove, but he could clear the floor, put old tins and packets into cardboard boxes, stack them against the wall. There was no shortage of boxes. He spread old blankets across the chairs to cover the holes. Why not? The boy was bringing new ones.

He found eating difficult as the time drew near. There

was a sticky, metallic taste in his mouth that no amount of tea or soup could wash away. A pressure seemed to be building in his head which made his thoughts distant, as if they were being squeezed through a narrow, constricted space. Rather like that time he had nailed himself to the table; only this time he didn't want the relief of that. When the sensation became intense he went outside and broke up pallets. The exercise was distracting.

On the Sunday he waited for the church bells and, as they rang, felt the chimes jangle inside his empty belly. He forced himself to eat two tablespoonfuls of sugar, straight from the bag, for his lunch. You had to keep your energy up.

He practised using his voice. Cleared his throat, coughed, to make sure his airways were clear. Said his own name, Harry. Easy. Harry. Harry. Then Joe. The 'o' noise pulled unnaturally at his lower jaw. Jo-o. Then Lizzie. Just a flick of the tongue. A hum in his throat. Lizzie. Like a saw buzzing. And finally Neil. Neil. The word sounded like an order. A natural, authoritative sound. Neil. His voice, saying it, gained confidence and strength.

He was listening out today and heard the car draw up out on the lane. He went to stand in the hallway. The knock was more a scrape; the boy must have his hands full. He opened the door. There was a pile of blankets over the boy's shoulder and his arms were wide with box.

'Here you are then, Mr Daniels.' That smile flashed at him again. 'Blankets too. Told you I wouldn't forget.'

Harry nodded at him and, though it took huge effort, breaking the habit of thirty years, stepped aside.

'Oh right. Take them in, shall I?' The boy looked surprised, but pleased.

Harry nodded again and, as the boy passed with his load, reached down his right leg for the wooden handle of the axe. He made a grunting noise when the boy tried to go the wrong way, into the back kitchen, and the boy glanced behind him and obeyed the jerk of his head by turning into the living room.

'Ooh, Mr Daniels, it's cold in here.' Neil humped the box on to the table. He slid the blankets from his shoulder on to the back of one of the chairs. Then stared around. His lips pursed and a small line creased the skin between his eyebrows. 'You managing all right, Mr Daniels?' His voice had become faint, as if it was hard to speak and look at the same time. 'Oh, Mr Daniels. I don't need to rush off. Can I do anything for you?'

Harry knew he did want the boy to do something, or to do something with the boy, but couldn't remember what. He was mesmerized by the boy's appearance. So fresh and pure, standing there in his grey sweatshirt with a hood at the back, his blue jeans. And his face: the beauty of his profile, the sweep of his silky hair, the glint of gold at his ear. The boy's eyes had reached the window and halted, resting on the hanging dress. His lips parted, but he said nothing.

'Lizzie,' Harry said. The blue material reminded him. That was why the boy was here, because of Lizzie.

'Is he what?' The boy pulled his eyes from the dress. He looked puzzled, but eager to understand.

'Lizzie,' said Harry again.

'Oh, *Lizzie*. Sorry, Mr Daniels. Who's Lizzie?'

The boy was a good actor. *Who's Lizzie.* Harry thought he was going to choke. But the anger cleared his mind. That was why he had brought the boy inside, to show him he knew. To expose their machinations, their conspiracy. He realized, suddenly, the purpose of the dress. The boy was their tool, their weapon. He dared to impersonate Lizzie. Well, let him do it properly. That would show them.

'Put it on,' he said.

'I'm sorry?' The boy peered at him, at a loss.

'The frock,' he said. 'Put it on.'

The boy pulled back, half laughed. 'Oh, Mr Daniels, I don't think it would suit me, do you?' His mouth dipped in and out of a smile.

'Put it on,' Harry repeated, and took a step towards him. He lifted his arm, just an inch or two.

The boy noticed the axe for the first time. His eyes widened, darted sideways. 'I think I have to go now, Mr Daniels,' he murmured, his body shifting. 'I'll leave you in peace.'

Harry stared at him. The boy tucked his chin into his chest and walked past him, making for the doorway. The moment his back was fully turned Harry swung the axe upright, the blunt side of the head foremost, and hit him with it between the shoulder blades.

The boy staggered, made a noise like someone blowing a pea-less whistle, and dropped to his knees. Then tipped forward on to his hands. Harry walked over to the hanging dress, yanked it down, and tossed it across the boy's back.

'Put it on.'

The boy didn't respond. Harry moved round to his head, to stand between him and the doorway. The boy's golden hair was hanging forward, hiding his face. A weakling, to fall like that. He hadn't used a fraction of his full strength.

Slowly the boy lifted his head. His complexion was white, his eyelashes fluttering. 'Mr Daniels,' he whispered. 'Jesus . . . Please . . .'

Harry prodded the boy's shoulder with the head of the axe. Then pushed, hard, forcing him back on his heels. The boy's hands scrabbled at the axe, so he snatched it back again.

'Mr Daniels.' The boy's voice was shaking. 'I'm Neil. You know, Dad's . . . Joe's son . . .'

Harry swung the axe backwards, underarm, and let its own weight carry it back. The head hit the front of the boy's knee.

'Jesus Christ!' This time the boy shot upright, back into the room, staggering and stumbling, grabbing at his leg. He came to rest leaning against the back of one of the blanket-covered arm chairs. Harry scooped up the dress and threw it at him. It landed on the chair back, only inches from the boy's hands. But still he didn't take it. Harry stepped forward and lifted the axe again.

The boy glanced quickly back at him, and seemed to go into a frenzy. He wrenched at his sweatshirt, snatching it off over his head. He was wearing a T-shirt underneath, with words on it that made no sense to Harry; he ripped this off too. He fumbled with the zip at the back of the dress, pulling at the tag, again and again, shaking his head.

'I can't . . . Mr Daniels, I can't, please, it's stuck.'

'Put it on.'

The boy's face screwed up. He started to cry. Thin muscles jerked under the white skin of his torso as he wept, struggling with the zip. He twisted towards the window for more light, and Harry saw the livid mark on his back, a dent rather than a swelling, stippled with darker dots, like a freckled hen's egg.

The zip gave. Harry heard the ratchet hiss of the teeth opening. Now the boy didn't know what to do, how to put a dress on. He raised it, lowered it again, flapped it helplessly. Then, with a sob, kicked his shoes off – ugly, clumsy, sports shoes – undid his belt, and wrestled off his jeans. He was wearing bright red underpants beneath, very brief and tight, like women's panties. He stepped into the dress, swivelled it around him, and tugged it up over his narrow hips. He pushed his arms through the armholes and pulled the front up. Then stood motionless, his head bowed, forearms resting on the chair, his bare back towards Harry.

'Do it up,' Harry said.

The boy nodded, without turning. His hands crept behind his back, over his hips, fingers searching for the zip. The material was rucked inside itself; even when he found the tag he had difficulty moving it. A little way above his waist he gave up.

'I can't do it,' he whispered. He was standing so still he seemed to be vibrating.

Harry walked over to him, pulled the rucks out of the material, and tugged the zip up. The freckled bruise disappeared beneath the blue material. At the top he had to touch the boy's hair, lifting it out of the way. It was soft and fine and smelt of soap. He remembered doing this for Lizzie. Under his fingers the boy's skin shivered. He stepped back.

'Turn round,' he said, and heard his voice gruff and thick.

The boy turned. The dress gave him a waist. It was short, shorter than it had been on Lizzie, reaching only half-way down his thighs. His naked arms were white and slender, though their shape was more sculpted, more muscular than hers. The boy stood awkwardly, his weight resting on his uninjured leg. He lifted his head, blinked his long, wet eyelashes, and stared off somewhere into the corner of the room.

'Mr Daniels,' he said in a very small voice. 'Please don't touch me. Please let me go.'

The boy was mimicking her. Even in defeat. Even now their game was exposed. Her voice, her words. Next he would be saying he had a pain in his belly.

The boy gave a small cough and winced. 'I don't feel very well, Mr Daniels. I think you've hurt me.' He coughed again and a spot of bright red froth appeared at the corner of his mouth. He touched the side of his hand to it, and then stared at the hand.

Lizzie had not bled from the mouth. She had not bled from anywhere visible. Not even from her woman's parts, though the doctors said this was unusual. She had vomited, at some time during the evening, but not bled. All her split blood had stayed inside her, formed that cruel, grotesque swelling in her abdomen. But earlier, when he had been with her, there had been nothing to see. Just the sweat on her skin, which he had put down to the summer heat, and her temper. And the pain, which he had not believed.

The boy tried to say something else, but coughed instead. He had to steady himself on the chair. White face, bright cherry lips.

She had been extraordinarily white. When he had unlocked the bedroom door, after she had been quiet for a couple of hours, that was the first thing that struck him. How white she had become. Then he had smelt, and seen, the vomit on the floor under the window, and then he had failed to rouse her.

The boy's legs were buckling; he was going to fall. Harry let the axe drop and stepped forward to grasp him by the upper arms. The boy moaned and his shoulders convulsed, trying to pull away. Maybe the grip hurt him. As gently as he could Harry lowered him to the floor. He laid him on his back, straightened his limbs. The boy's body was rigid, but unresisting. Harry reached for one of the new blankets, shook it out, and spread it over him.

If he had realized she was ill, he could have saved her. If he had believed her, he could have saved her. A few hours, they said, would have made all the difference. *It's like a nail going through me, Harry,* she had screamed. *Like a nail. I have to see the doctor.* And he had ignored her, because he'd heard it all before. He had locked the bedroom door on her, gone downstairs, and turned the television on, so her voice was just a distant wail in the lulls.

This was the test. Harry suddenly realized it. The knowledge shocked him, but there was no doubt about it. Joe was a cruel, ruthless man. Prepared to risk his son's life, to avenge his aunt's. Poor Neil. Poor Lizzie. Stiffly he knelt down and touched the boy's face, which was cool under his fingertips. The boy's eyelashes lifted, then closed tight again. He was trembling, his breathing shallow, but perhaps more afraid than hurt. He was just bleeding, a little, in his lungs. The sight of his own blood, perhaps, had frightened him. The blow on his back must have been harder than he'd intended, must have broken something. A rib, maybe. A sharp, puncturing rib. Harry had seen such things before, at the steel works.

And he knew what to do. He remembered what to do. The boy shouldn't be lying down. If there was blood in his lungs, he could drown in it. He must sit up. He worked an arm under the boy's shoulders, ignored the shuddering, the shrinking away, and lifted his upper body. Propped him against the chair back. Wedged him in place with blankets.

There. He sat back on his heels. He felt huge pity for the boy. Anger on his behalf. Joe had used his son. He had been lucky enough to have a son, and did not value him. Saw him only as bait. If he, Harry, had had a son – a son or daughter – he would have valued the child. His child, the doctors said, had been only the size of a tadpole when it burst out of its faulty resting place, its tiny constricting tube, killing itself, and mortally wounding its mother. A tadpole. Only eight weeks old. They hadn't even known she was pregnant.

He patted the boy's cheek again – Lizzie's cheek, he

thought, the same flesh, the same essence – and grunted, 'It's all right. You'll be all right.' The boy whimpered and turned his face away, pushing it into the greasy filth of the chair back. Harry reached for the axe and leant on the handle to lever himself upright. 'Next door,' he said. 'A telephone. Don't worry.'

He left the room, and then the cottage. He opened the gate, and stepped out on to the lane. There was a breeze, blowing fresh dampness into his face. Across the small dividing field he could see his neighbour's wife already, at the side of the bungalow, her rubber-booted foot pressing a fork into the dark earth of their vegetable patch. He walked towards her, practising sounds in his head, shaping the words they would make. And, as he did so, felt a deep, triumphant sense of pride. He would pass the test. Words, from him to her, in time to save a precious life.

TIMES LIKE THIS

'Come on, Mum.' Angela leant impatiently into her mother's kitchen, rattling her car keys. 'Jenny and the baby won't wait.'

Sylvia picked up her purse from the back of the work surface. What rubbish. In her experience babies – first babies – were rarely in a rush. Purse, book, reading glasses, better take her indigestion pills, too. Goodness knows how long this could take . . .

Her daughter came further into the room. Cropped hair, large-boned naked face. Faint shadows at the corners of her upper lip. Fifty-five last birthday. She looked, Sylvia thought, with sudden viciousness, more and more like a man.

The angles of Angela's face softened. 'Are you all right, Mum?'

'Of course I am.'

'You don't need to dress up, you know. It's only a hospital.'

Sylvia bit back a caustic reply. She was not 'dressed up'. Just because she took the trouble to do her face, groom herself, before stepping out into the world. Angela was wearing a pair of baggy cotton trousers that did absolutely nothing for her backside. Buttocks like sandbags. Didn't she ever use a mirror? No wonder Ken had left her. No. She shook her head. Dear me. Dear me. That was *so* unfair. What was wrong with her? All week she had felt irritable, disorganised . . .

'I've got magazines in the car. And snacks. In case there's no canteen. You might look keener, Mum. Honestly, Jenny's going to really appreciate this.'

Sylvia sighed. Her daughter knew – what was that expression? – yes, 'which button to push'. That soft one, called granddaughter. Although she bet this was more Angela's idea than Jenny's. Young women these days didn't go in for 'sisterly' gestures, demonstrations, did they?

She followed Angela out of the front door and across the concrete paving to the Volvo. She gave a little wave to Jocelyn, her neighbour, who was sitting in the bay window of her bungalow just yards away. Poor Jocelyn. A heart condition and terrible legs. And only sixty-eight.

Neither mother nor daughter spoke until they'd negotiated the bends of the estate and they were out on the ring road. Then, stretching her arms and sitting back in the driver's seat Angela said, 'I rang you a dozen times Monday, during the day, but I couldn't catch you. Sorry, I had to go out in the evening.'

'I was at the church most of the afternoon. Obviously. They've got a goat in there now, you know, to eat the grass. Horrible slitty eyes. Quite inappropriate. And messing all over the place.'

'Why don't you get an answer-phone, Mum? Or a mobile?'

'Don't be silly.'

'You can get an answering service through the exchange. It's all set up for you, you don't have to plug anything in. Costs pennies.'

'Your father and I managed fifty years without any of these things. Why should I want them now?'

Angela said nothing but jabbed at the indicator stalk. Sylvia heard the rhythmic clicking. *So we can check up on you now you're old and alone.* That's what her daughter wasn't saying. So ruddy tactful.

'I was thinking of Dad, anyway,' Angela sighed, straightening up the car after the turn. There was a large red H on a signpost in front of them. 'That's all I wanted to tell you.'

'I couldn't see any point in leaving flowers,' Sylvia said. 'Not with that goat around.'

'He'd have been eighty, wouldn't he?'

'Angela. D'you have to ask?'

'No, of course not. Obviously.' She sighed again. 'What I mean is that you'll be eighty, too, at the end of the year. Jenny and I were talking about it. We wondered if you'd like a party.'

'A party? Goodness me, no. Of course not. Eighty. What on earth is there to celebrate about being eighty?'

'Well . . . your life. Your amazing good health. I don't know. Lots of people have eightieths. It's a family thing.'

'A family thing. And what family have I got?'

'Oh Mum. Don't be like that.'

It's true, though, Sylvia thought savagely. Look at us. Our family. Start with me. A mother who bears two children, a son and a daughter, the son dying of meningitis at the age of six (oh, you are not forgotten, Richard, my sweet Richard). The surviving child, Angela, grows up and marries a charming but hopeless man, Ken, and, after two miscarriages, bears her own daughter. Just the one child. She doesn't push her luck. Then, the moment that only child is adult, she and her husband divorce. Husband disappears to somewhere in Scotland. And now Jenny, loving, clever, beautiful grandchild that she is, hasn't bothered to get married at all. Doesn't propose even to live with the father of her child. Dear God. Perhaps it was better that Edward didn't live to see this day, the birth of his first, fatherless great-grandchild.

'Ken'll be down tomorrow, hopefully,' Angela said. 'He may have to hire a car, because his is playing up. Honestly, I wish he'd get his life sorted. And Jenny's rung Tim. Just before she went in. I told you her waters had broken, didn't I? Going up the steps to the flat. Lucky it wasn't a few minutes earlier, in Sainsbury's. He's going to ring me back tonight. Or whatever time it is in New York. He sounds very excited.'

Tim was the father. A man Sylvia had yet to meet. An American who worked in banking. As did Jenny. Both earned ludicrous salaries. She couldn't stop herself saying, not for the first time, 'How will she manage, all on her own . . .?'

'Mum.' Angela's tone was weary.

'Handing it over to a nanny. Poor little mite.'

'It's what people in Jenny's world do, Mum. If they do it at all. Half of her friends think she's mad to have kids, full stop. The other half are going to wait till they're forty.'

'A child needs a father. Wasn't your father important to you?'

'Of course. Incredibly. But I didn't see much of him when I was small, did I? You used to send me to bed at half past six. She's not writing Tim out of her life, Mum. They're devoted to each other. He's over here at least six weeks a year. And she'll go over there.'

'Six weeks a year.'

'Things might change. Who knows what'll happen?'

'We were a real family. Your father worked for us. Allowed me to look after you properly. Ken did the same for you. You had at least five years off with Jenny.'

'And we were practically destitute. It's just not possible these days, Mum. Not for the way people want to live, anyway.'

'Because they're greedy,' said Sylvia. 'Because they want everything.'

They had had these arguments before. Pigheaded, pointless arguments. Evidence of proof was overwhelming, on both sides. Look at the terrible behaviour of even quite small children these days, Sylvia would say, admit the crassness of youth. All the fault of the modern, selfish, materialistic, neglectful family. Breeding unhealthy, philistine, greedy children, umbilically attached to their computer games, designer clothes, mobile phones and inhalers. Whose only ambitions were to be rich and famous, which they expected to achieve with no hard work or sacrifice. You're being quite unfair, Angela would protest. Think of the children you know. I know. Actually *know*, not just heard about. All those resourceful, independent kids travelling the world at eighteen, twenty, gaining a broadening glimpse of other lives. More of them at university than ever before, working harder than ever before. Most of them friends, yes, friends, with their parents. Not like a generation ago. Look around at the real world, Mum. Families are as good now as they've ever been.

How reasonable Angela was these days. How tolerant of the lifestyles of generations other than her own. How unlike the passionate, virulent Angela of twenty five, thirty years ago. The young woman who had tried to persuade herself, Sylvia, that she was hard done by. Suggesting that Edward, working ten hours a day sometimes at the Revenue offices, was somehow oppressing her. While she, Sylvia, did her part-time school job, loving every minute, and with all that left-over time to herself. How, Sylvia would demand, could it be a triumph for women, now, to take on the slaving lifestyles they once despised, the lifestyles of men? It was obviously failure, not triumph. And if Angela had known then that one day she would have a daughter in banking . . . heavens, Angela wouldn't have worked for *any* private business in her youth, never mind one dedicated to money.

'I can't get my head round the idea of being a grand-mother.' Angela was smiling goofily into the windscreen.

Sylvia, despite her mood, was touched by her daughter's expression. Really, Angela was an innocent. 'It is a pleasure,' she murmured. 'It is. A joy.'

'I hope so,' said Angela.

Sylvia couldn't resist adding, 'It would have been nice to have more . . .'

'Mmm.' Angela didn't appear to take this as criticism. 'We haven't had much luck with children, really, have we?'

This was such an intimate remark, never before expressed, and said now so casually, that it made Sylvia breathless. Ashamed of herself. Of course, miscarriages weren't the same as losing a grown child, but loss was still loss. Suddenly alarmed, she said, 'Jenny's been well, though, hasn't she?'

'Oh yes. Don't worry. Strong as an ox. Ridiculously fertile, you know. Only gave up the pill two months before she got pregnant. And blooming now. I think she's got your constitution, Mum.'

Oh, Sylvia sighed to herself, Angela is so generous, forgiving. She thought of apologizing: *don't mind me, dear, I'm just a crabby old thing.*

But then her daughter cried, 'Look, here we are!'

'Mum! Gran! Come in, come in!' The pink-cheeked young woman in the bed gave a cry of delight, and then a laughing sob.

'Darling . . .' Angela rushed towards her. 'Are you all right . . .?'

'Of course I am. Of course.' She embraced her mother, then held her arms out to Sylvia. 'Oh Gran, Gran. Give us a hug.'

Sylvia let herself be enfolded, kissed the soft wet cheek of her granddaughter. Impossible to believe that this child was twenty-eight. Straight, sleek, school-girl hair that in Angela's day would have been held back with a slide or Alice band. A quick, mobile face. Expressive, optimistic, unreserved. Cried over anything. Bounced back like a baby. She travelled to work in a business suit and trainers.

'I'm so bored between contractions. There's another woman who came in the same time and she's still walking round outside, but her waters haven't gone. It's unusual, apparently, for it to be the first thing that happens. But the midwife says it'll probably make it quicker. She's absolutely lovely, Myrtle. The midwife. Silly name, isn't it, Myrtle. Like turtle. Sorry I'm gabbling on, but I'm so glad you're here. Myrtle thinks it's wonderful, having a mum and gran with me.' She winced. 'Oh God . . .' Grasping the base of her huge gown-covered abdomen, she closed her eyes. 'Here goes,' she hissed. 'Sorry folks.'

Angela pulled up a couple of cushioned chairs, one either side of the bed. As she sat down Sylvia noticed a lumpy mound of what looked like bean bags in the corner of the room. Those silly noisy slumping seats that young people used to buy. Of course, women these days were allowed to undergo labour how they liked. Wallowing in birthing pools. Rolling on bean bags, walking the hospital grounds. Jenny was probably unusual in choosing a conventional bed. They watched her puff her way through the contraction.

'I thought you were going to have an epidural?' Angela said cautiously, as Jenny's head sagged back on the huge heap of pillows.

'Changed my mind. Read up more about it. Phew, they're strong though. And it can only get worse, can't it? Never mind.' She pulled her heavy body awkwardly up the mattress. 'I'm sure I'll manage. Myrtle says it may only be a couple of hours, or less. I'm three quarters dilated already.'

'Really? God.' Angela smiled at her daughter admiringly. 'You look so in control. When I was at the same stage with you I was zonked out with pethidine.'

'They have offered me something, actually, but I said I wanted to be clear-headed later. Well, it was easy to say no then.' Impulsively Jenny reached for Sylvia's hand and squeezed it. 'I'm so glad you're here, Gran. The three of us. You had Mum at home, didn't you? What was that like?'

Sylvia shook her head. 'Um . . . I remember it as easy. But I don't suppose it was really. You forget.' Something incidental came back to her. 'Oh yes. The downstairs of that little house stank afterwards, I remember that. The doctor came round to chat to the midwife about something – I never saw him myself – and he chain-smoked. Dreadful man. The room stank for days.'

'Wow,' Jenny sighed. 'Unbelievable.'

A tall black woman with an aristocratically high forehead and beaded swept-back hair strode into the room.

'And how is my Jenny now?' She smiled broadly at Angela and Sylvia. 'Ah, so this is your mother and grand-mother – how very nice to meet you. I'm looking after your young lady and she is a healthy girl who is having no troubles at all. She has a great big bottom and if I were her I would have dozens of babies.'

'Oh shut up, Myrtle,' said Jenny.

Myrtle chuckled. 'Very soon you will all have a lovely infant.'

'It's going to be a girl,' said Jenny.

'Sorry?' said Sylvia, alert.

'Now you don't know that,' said Myrtle, wagging her finger at Jenny. 'She is full of superstition, your little girl.'

'The woman measured its head,' Jenny said. 'At the scan.'

'Really?' said Angela eagerly. 'They can tell from that?'

'They can tell nothing,' said Myrtle. 'Not unless they see a winkle. Heads, pah. These days, the boys are little things and the girls, well, they have big fat heads.' She laughed throatily.

'And someone said because of where I'm carrying it . . .'

'You're talking nonsense. It will be what it will be. Now . . .' Myrtle turned to Sylvia and Angela. 'I must examine your little girl. I know she looks as comfortable as someone wasting our time, but actually she is close. Very close. Just a lucky girl.'

Sylvia picked up her handbag. Angela hesitated, then said, 'Of course, we'll leave you.'

'No, Mummy!' Jenny cried. 'Stay with me!'

'Only one in the delivery suite,' Myrtle sang. 'You know that, poppet, don't you.'

'Oh darling . . .' Angela looked torn.

'I'll be perfectly all right,' said Sylvia briskly. 'I've brought my book. Of course your mother must be with you.'

'There's a coffee shop . . .' said Angela.

'I know. I saw it. I'm not incapable.'

Sylvia made do with a cup of horrible stewed tea from the kiosk at Outpatients. The coffee actually smelt quite appetizing, but even the mildest decaffeinated brew could give her indigestion these days, so she daren't risk it. Still: predictable indigestion, a nobby clutch of arthritic fingers, and a mild right-eye cataract – not bad for seventy-nine. She walked back to the ground-floor maternity unit down a warren of corridors. Good thing her feet were healthy. But it was alarming the way people coming towards her barged open the swing doors. You'd think in a hospital they'd be more careful. Rush rush rush. Everyone these days in a rush.

Back in Maternity, large glass doors off the waiting area had been slid open onto a small, shrub-encircled garden. Sylvia inspected it from the doorway. Could have been a pretty spot, if it hadn't been littered with cigarette stubs. The shrubs were in flower – Hebes, with blue blossoms like lambs' tails. To think that once Hebes had been considered exotic; a municipal standard, these days. There was a wooden bench on the grass, solid, with a high seat and straight back. She walked over to it, careful not to dent the turf with her small heels, and, grasping the seat arm, lowered herself on to the seat. Oh yes. Much easier than the low plastic-padded chairs inside.

She would stay here a while. Not rush back. Jenny was about to have the baby, that was clear. She didn't feel strong enough to see Jenny distressed. Such powerful, chaotic urges – she recalled experiencing them herself. Overwhelmed with, what? – pain? frustration? – and using language – well, be honest, expletives – she would have been ashamed, afterwards, to admit she knew. She'd been glad Edward hadn't been there.

These days, of course, husbands, no, *partners*, were everywhere. No privacy, even in childbirth. Goodness – she immediately shifted position to sit more upright – there was a man here now, just stepping out into the garden. Aged about forty, check shirt and overwashed blue jeans. But a sensible, weather-beaten face. Robust build. Actually quite attractive. Someone who might be a competent, *responsible* man.

He was lighting up a cigarette, cupping a hand to his face against the breeze. As he took his first long draw he grinned across at Sylvia. She was momentarily astonished – did she know him? no, of course she didn't – and then, even more astonishingly, felt herself responding. A surge of goodwill.

'It's a girl,' the man announced, his face split by his

smile. 'At long bloody last.' He walked across to the bench. She could feel his excitement like a heat around him.

'Congratulations. I'm sorry, a bit of a trial for your wife, was it?'

The man laughed. He sounded slightly delirious. 'Christ no. Pops 'em like peas. But this is the fifth. All the rest boys. God, we wanted a girl.'

'Oh,' said Sylvia. Five children. Gracious. 'What a big family,' she said. 'How very nice.'

The man indicated the space on the bench to Sylvia's right. 'D'you mind?' He waved his cigarette. 'Should be a cigar. Sorry. Meant to have given up. Such a relief.' He slumped down on the wood and grinned dreamily. 'Last time we go through this, thank God.'

'Four boys,' murmured Sylvia.

'Aye. Great lads. Great. But my wife's sister, she's got two. And my brother, three. When they're together, Christ, it's bedlam.'

'We don't have any boys in our family.' The words came out like something she had been bursting to say for days. 'Just a daughter and granddaughter. The girl . . . she's the one having the baby.'

'Done away with the lads, eh?' the man laughed. 'Bet it's a smooth-run ship, then.'

He laughed. How strange. As if it were funny. As if a family without men could be viable, acceptable. No threat. *Done away with the lads.*

'Well, it's women keep families going, isn't it? That's what the wife says, anyroad. Someone who'll pick up a phone now and then.' He chuckled, half apologetically. 'And every dad wants his little girl, doesn't he?'

Well, thought Sylvia, that isn't strictly true. Angela used to rant about this. In some parts of the world, evidently, girls weren't wanted at all. But yes, oh yes, Edward had adored Angela, his little girl. Even when she was a young adult, so spiky and difficult. There had always been a bond. Akin to true love. Like between herself and Edward. Or herself and Richard. Oh dear. These invading, upsetting thoughts.

'Your granddaughter's had a little girl too, then?' the man asked.

'What?' Sylvia gathered herself. 'No, no . . . she hasn't had it yet. We'll have to see. Her mother's with her now. Her . . . partner's in the States, just at the moment.'

'You want a little boy, then, do you, for all you ladies to dote on?'

Did she? Oh, yes, just thinking it made her heart leap. How she yearned for the touch, the scent, of a boy, a man. Replacement of what was lost. But would it be right, in her family? Would a boy be safe? Goodness, what a morbid, superstitious thought. Her emotions were all over the place. Had been all week. She reminded herself: the baby was Jenny's, not for her or Angela. And what the man said was true: daughters were forever.

'I don't think we mind,' she said firmly. 'As long as the baby's healthy.'

'That's the way,' the man said. He chuckled ruefully. 'But you wait till it's the fifth.'

Sylvia sighed. Five children. All those boys, and the girl, strong healthy young branches. Unendangered. Green and thriving. A family that would blossom.

'It'll be my first great-grandchild,' she said.

'Hey!' He swung to look at her. He had lovely blue eyes. 'Must be a proud moment. Your husband, he here too?'

'Oh, no. No. I'm afraid Edward . . . my . . . um . . . he passed on, well, nearly two years ago.'

'Oh, my.' The eyes winced. 'I'm sorry to hear that. Very sorry. My mum didn't get to see the last boy. Pretty sudden

. . . just a couple of months before. Crippled me, and me Dad. It's times like this, isn't it?'

'Yes.' She fixed her eyes on the blue flowers across the grass. Edward had had lovely eyes, too. She heard herself saying, 'He would have been eighty this week.' Times like this. Moments like this. Birth and death. She got up suddenly. 'I think I must go and see what's happening.' She held out her hand. 'Please give my congratulations to your wife.' As she squeezed his firm, masculine hand she imagined embracing him. Inhaling him. He wasn't Edward, of course. But a man was a man. Goodness, he'd be shocked. She almost laughed. What a silly old woman she was.

As she turned the corner into the long maternity corridor she saw Angela the far end, striding towards her. A band of tension dropped from her chest – it was over, the baby born. She could tell from the energy in her daughter's body, the long, excited strides.

'Mum!' Angela cried, spotting her. 'It's a boy, a beautiful little boy! Oh Mum!' Now she was actually running towards Sylvia. Her bosom bounding. What a ridiculous, ungainly sight.

'Steady, steady,' Sylvia said gruffly, bracing herself as Angela flung her arms around her. 'You'll have me over.'

'Oh, Mum,' sobbed Angela. 'A little boy. Oh Mum.' Her cheek was pressed hard against Sylvia's ear.

Sylvia held her daughter. 'There, there,' she murmured. 'There, there.' She patted the heaving back. What a to do. What a fuss. But perhaps Angela was missing Edward too. Dear me. Of course she would be. His little girl. Oh, times like this.

PRIMROSE HILL

He shouldn't have touched my head. First thing, I tell them that. Well, second thing. Forty quid, I say – the price tells them what they're getting – and no one touches my head. No one. He'd opened the passenger door of the Audi, reaching across from the driver's seat, and I saw his eyes looking me up and down, hearing me. Then he nodded and said, 'Climb in, son.' Definitely heard me. Fuck him.

Shit, it's a steep pull up here, especially when you're running. My heart's beating so fierce I can feel it in my feet, like the ground's pulsing. But I've made it. And it's worth it when you turn round. Brings tears to your eyes – na, only kidding; it's the wind. London. Looks like . . . somewhere really hard to leave. The lights pull and wink at you. She's an ugly old bag, close to, or in daylight, but at night she's all dolled up and the jewellery glints. You don't see the rest, even when it's right beside you, like Mr Audi down there, opening its wallet.

Here's the notice board. Too dark to read, but I know what's on it. There's a jagged wiggle across the brass plate like one of those electrical games, those tests of hand-control that buzz if you touch the wire. The wiggle's the skyline. Canary Wharf on the left, can't remember what's on the right. St Paul's, Telecom Tower, all sorts in between.

It's for tourists, so they can put names to what they're looking at. I know all the landmarks now. Sky marks, they should be called. And down below's the Zoo, just at the bottom of the hill, before London starts. So dark I can't really see it. Just the top of those weird-shaped bird-cages. Between me and London's the Zoo. Quite funny, that.

Primrose Hill. Nice name – like it's in the country, and it's always springtime. Primrose Hill. So uncool it's cool. I once ate primroses. With my cousins, back in Cinderford. The only time I've ever picked flowers, honest guv. They grew on banks at the edge of the Forest. Tight curly veined leaves, like little cabbages, and sometimes you'd get a clump with pink flowers, determined to be flashier than the rest. Eating primroses sounds crazy but we were kids; nothing seemed crazy to us. Someone said they were edible, so we put the flowerheads between slices of bread and butter, sprinkled them with sugar, and scoffed them down. Not much taste, over the sugar, but they were OK. Mind you, I've been up here loads of time now, and I've never seen any primroses. Perhaps I've never been here in the springtime.

Close to, you can see all the car lights. Thousands and thousands of them. Red and white, all on the move. Wink zip flare. One set might be his: Mr Audi, Mr Fucking-can't-keep-his-hands-to-himself. He's that one, no, that one. Anyway, he's the one going fastest, as if his life depends on it. Which it might. Shit. Thinking that's given me the shakes; I got to sit down. But even if he can't drive he could press the horn. Yeah, the horn. He'd got the ignition on. As I scarpered he was firing the engine up. Someone'll hear it, and deal with him.

I flew so easily over the railings; must have been the adrenaline. I wonder if they patrol the Hill at night? Na. Lock the gates and forget about it. I hope. I can't go home yet. Give it a couple of hours. The wetness on my chest is stiffening.

Maybe I'll never know what I've done. I'll wait here till it's as quiet as it ever gets, dump the shirt in a bin – oh shit, it's the Ben Sherman, cost me sixty quid – and leg it back to Camden. And maybe nothing will happen. As if nothing did happen. Except I got pictures in my head. Him roaring through the traffic, knowing his London, screeching up outside Accident and Emergency – Royal Free, I'm imagining – leaning on the horn. Or maybe he'll see a police car, stop it somehow, and they'll sort him out. Or anyone. He'd only have to make it to a main road.

Or maybe he didn't go anywhere at all, but is still parked in the side-road, the engine chugging, bleaching white under the red, going slowly to sleep.

I don't care. I don't fucking care. My head's my own. Don't want anyone fucking with it. What I do is down to me; I'm not having any pervert thinking otherwise. It's not much to ask. My head stays free.

Inside his wallet he had a string of plastic cards. Credit cards, store cards, smart cards. A dozen or more of them. He wanted me to see them. And the wad of twenties. Peeled off just two of them. He got a kick from showing me how cheap I was. Fucking wanker. That's arrogant. It's saying, you're nothing, boy, but look what I am, what I can buy. It assumes I'm no threat, I'm someone you can flaunt cards and notes at, and walk away from. I'm that puny, that insignificant. I got a right to be mad.

But I didn't take the wallet, and I'm glad I didn't. I could have, while he was panicking, while he was still grappling with his leg and his trousers. I could be sitting here now with a pack of plastic, and a fistful of twenties. But I think I'll feel better about it later, tomorrow, next week, next year, knowing I didn't take it. Keeping myself in the right. Sticking to my own rules. Not fucking up the issue. One day I won't be doing this. That's why I want no legacies, nothing to remind me, nothing to regret. When the time comes, when I can afford it, when I choose to do it, I'll make a clean break.

I reckon he put his hand on my head for the same reason he showed me his wallet. A sad bastard. He takes shit at work, or at home, so he comes cruising up here to give shit to us. He heard what I told him, but I'm nothing, so what I said didn't count. He was buying the willingness to take shit. He thought.

I may have killed him. No. Yeah. I'd like to know. Killing someone would be a kind of legacy. Something you could never put right. Even if I didn't mean to. You got to carry a blade, but I didn't plan where it went. How could I? He had his hands on my head. It's not a long blade, must have been a chance in a thousand. There's monsters out there, you got to have protection. I tape it to my wrist. Just a press on the spring, and a quick jab in the thigh. In and out, fast as that. Can't have gone in more than an inch. Just to fucking stop him. But for a moment I thought I'd cut a heater hose, the liquid was so warm and spurting.

If he's dead they'll come looking. I got his blood on my clothes and on the blade. If he didn't make it out of the side-road, there'll be sirens. I'd hear them up here. Someone'll find him – engine running, passenger door open. I've heard nothing so far. No horn, no sirens. Not close, anyway. He must have got away, and if he got away, he'll have got help, and he's not dead. And if he's not dead, I'm safe. I didn't rob him. No punter brings charges. But I need to know. I want no legacies. I want to keep my slate clean, and my head straight. I'll give it an hour, watching the old tart sprawled in her finery the other side of the Zoo. Think primroses a while. Just to be sure.

BARBECUE

It's Saturday morning and we're headed north out of Beaufort, out of the Valleys, up on to the mountain. Jaz on his Guzzi, Mitch on his Triumph chop, and me on the Z1000, on our way to Crickhowell for a drink. And to get away from our mate Dai, who's panicking back at the field because the others haven't returned from Glastonbury with the bus, and how the hell is he going to lay on a barbecue this evening without the cooking gear?

Not a soul on the mountain but we can't open up the bikes for the hordes of sheep dawdling on the tarmac, bleating and giving us the idiot eye. They've got half a county of moorland to roam across, up here, but as usual they're ignoring it. Mitch reckons it's definite proof of over-civilisation, when even the sheep are scared of getting lost.

The other side of the mountain, and we're into Tourist Information Wales. Money and horseboxes and hang-gliders and not a derelict factory in sight. The little town of Crickhowell, nestling snug and smug over the Usk.

We get to the pub and down a swift ale, and we're just explaining to the landlord about the bruises on Jaz's face when the door opens and who should fall through it but the bus crowd. That's Wayne, Pete, and the two girls.

'What you doing here?' Mitch bellows across the room

at them, making half the bar slop their pints. Short on manners, Mitch is, but the landlord's easygoing. 'Dai's doing his nut, waiting for you.'

The girls duck down the corridor to the Ladies and Pete and Wayne push their way towards us. Pete has got his hair tied back in a dinky plait, instead of loose and ratsy. Wayne is in his He-Man rig, bandannaed blonde mane over acres of leather-strapped tanned flesh. They stare at the purple lumps on Jaz's face with awe. Sharp little face, Jaz had, when they last saw him. Looks like a plum pudding now. 'Shit, man.' Pete looks alarmed. 'How's the Guzzi?'

Jaz tells him, like he was just telling the landlord, that the Guzzi's fine, but that he had a run-in with a couple of lads from Tredegar. Yesterday, it was. He sold them a Suzi, and it blew up before they reached Ebbw Vale. They wanted the Guzzi to make up for it, but he hid it in his mam's back kitchen and took a thumping on the doorstep instead.

Wayne claps him round the shoulders, making him flinch – thoughtful type, Wayne is – and says he'd have been safer at Glastonbury, where it was all peace and love and a soft landing on mud.

'You there all this time?' I ask. 'Been more than a week.'

'Na,' says Wayne. 'Trouble in Bristol coming back.' He grins wide. 'This publican, he won't serve us 'cos he says we're a coach party. So I backed over his fence, accidental-like, on the way out. The cops had us for criminal damage. Got a conditional discharge.'

Jaz wonders how many hospital visits it takes to cure a conditional discharge, and I tell Wayne how Dai's got it into his head about this barbecue and wants the bus back pronto. The bus is mobile HQ – as well as the cooking gear, everyone's got equipment and spares stashed in it.

'Be back this afternoon,' Wayne promises. 'It's down the lay-by now. Just got to pick up stuff for the girls.'

They disappear after a quick pint. We don't stay long either, because Jaz's getting anxious about leaving the Guzzi in the car park up the road. It's day-tripping weather and the High Street's already jumping with Valley's lads.

Nobody near the bikes though, except a couple of kiddies admiring the puddle of oil under Mitch's chop. Brit bikes need to sweat, Mitch says, he's a patriot. We decide we'll head back and give Dai the good news. We set off and I'm in front, revelling in the way the Z1000 powers up the gradients, when I see a dead sheep, lying at the side of the road. Fair-sized corpse, but definitely a lamb, not one of the scrawny ewes.

I flag the others down. There's no one else on the road.

'This fella weren't here when we came across,' I say. 'Did you see him?'

'He weren't here,' says Mitch. 'We'd have noticed.'

Jaz props the Guzzi and squats down to take a dekko. Barbecue, I'm beginning to think.

'How long you reckon he's been dead?' I say.

'How long you been dead?' Jaz asks the lamb, but it stays stum.

'Stick your finger up its arse,' I say. 'See if it's warm.'

'I'm not sticking my finger up any tup's bum,' Jaz says. But Mitch dismounts and says he'll do it, so he can tell his grand-children about it when he's old, and they refuse to believe he had a wild childhood.

He pokes his finger into the lamb and says it's warm. He looks up and grins. Jaz and I grin back. We're all thinking barbecue now.

We ponder what to do next. We can't cruise into town with a dead tup behind us – even with a jacket on it won't fool anyone.

We decide to dump it in a shallow ditch a few yards from the road and go back to Jaz's place for equipment. His mam's got a smallholding this side of town. They don't keep stock now, but there's any tool you want in the sheds.

When we get there we find Lizzie all a twitter because the two Tredegar lads have been back. Jaz's mam is Lizzie to everyone except Jaz. She says the boys didn't come to the house, but she saw them with another lad in a white van, parked down the track. Jaz takes her into the front room to calm her down, and so she doesn't see us rummaging in the back shed for the axe and knives and a couple of plastic feed bags.

'She alright?' Mitch asks, as Jaz joins us in the hallway on the way out. It's not just politeness, we all got time for Lizzie. 'Cos she's always got time for us, I suppose. Jaz says she's OK now, no need to worry.

We drive like vicars on mopeds out of town with the gear stuffed down our jackets, and pootle out to where we've hid the lamb.

There's a few cars on the road now. Mitch's the largest and ugliest of us so we leave him by the bikes to glare at anyone who looks like stopping, and Jaz and I scramble over the heather to the ditch.

We don't bother to skin the lamb, because Pete used to work in a slaughterhouse and can do it blindfold, we just chop off the head and feet and gut it. I'd have left the gore there for the foxes, but Jaz's fretting about an old ewe bleating at the edge of the ditch and says it's the tup's mam and we can't leave bits of her baby lying around. I say fine – you can't argue with Jaz about mother love – just so long as he deals with dumping it later. We stuff the carcass into one bag and the head and feet and as much of the guts as we can scrape up into the other. The carcass bag straps across the tank of the Z1000, and Jaz ties the other to the grab bar of the Guzzi. Then we drive, nice and sedate, the three miles through town to Dai's.

The bus is down the field already, next to Dai's collection of rotting mechanicals. But it's changed colour since last week. Instead of blue it's sickly green, with what look like white ticks round the windows. Down the field a bit the ticks turn out to be peace doves. We bounce the bikes over the grass to where Dai, Pete, and Pete's girlfriend Karin are standing by one of Dai's decomposing JCBs.

'What you done to the bus?' demands Mitch, as we prop the bikes. 'Bleeding hell.'

'You know anyone works in a chippie?' Dai asks, not listening. He still looks fraught, despite the return of the bus. He's tugging at clumps of his beard like he's plucking it. 'Need a sack of taters.'

'We got something better than taters,' Jaz says, beckoning him over to the bikes.

'Who painted the bus?' Mitch roars. 'Looks like a fucking playbus.'

'It was to get in,' Pete says soothingly. 'They said we could park it by the Green Field if we let the kids paint it.' He tilts his head and nods at it. 'Looks OK, I think.'

Behind his back Karin pulls a face and twists her finger into her temple. Dai's standing over the Z1000. 'Jeez,' he whistles, as Jaz opens the bag. 'Where'd you get that?'

'What is it?' asks Pete, coming over to look. He peers inside. 'Shit,' he says, stepping back.

'You got to skin it,' says Jaz. 'We done the rest.'

Pete shakes his head and says no way, he's become a vegetarian. But Karin rips into him and says she's fed up with him flirting with the hippies at the festival and if he wants to become a fairy that's up to him, but he's not sodding well laying it on us.

'OK, OK,' says Pete, with a look that suggests this isn't the first bollocking he's had over this, and agrees to skin the lamb as his last carnivorous act. Mitch gives him the axe and knives and he humps the bag up the field towards the outhouses. Karin follows him still giving him mouth.

'Where's Wayne?' I ask.

'In the bus with Josie,' says Dai. 'Better knock first.'

'My face hurts,' Jaz says, touching his cheek gingerly. 'I need a kip.'

'You got to dump that bag,' I remind him.

'Later,' he says.

I don't push it. He's suddenly looking very weary. He's holding his shoulders funny, and where the side of his helmet's been pressed against his cheekbone it's made a dent in one of the purple bruises. We walk over to the bus and Mitch kicks the side. Josie sticks her head out of a window, pulling a T-shirt on over her long straggly hair.

'Oi,' says Mitch. 'Jaz needs to kip.'

Josie says, 'Oh, right,' and there's some scuffling and groaning inside. She opens the back door tucking her T-shirt into her jeans. She looks at Jaz's face and winces. 'Better come inside,' she says. 'I got some aspirin.'

As they climb in Wayne hops out pulling on his boots. We start to move back to the bikes.

'You know the boys who did that?' Wayne gives a last hop and jerks his head back at the bus. He means Jaz's face. 'Any of you there?'

'Nope,' says Mitch. 'Just Jaz and Lizzie.'

'Uhuh,' says Wayne. I know what he's thinking. I'm beginning to think it too. It didn't sound so bad, the way Jaz told it, but who likes to tell it bad? And seeing how stiff the boy is, and mess they made of his face . . . it's out of order to thump a lad, and want his bike off him as well.

'They been round to his place again this morning,' I say, with my eyes on Wayne. 'They're after the Guzzi. Maybe they'll be back.'

Wayne picks up Jaz's helmet and climbs on to the pillion

of the Z1000. He grins, patting the seat in front of him. 'Let's go see,' he says.

Lizzie's pleased to see the three of us, especially when we tell her Jaz's fine, resting in the bus. She says she hasn't seen the Tredegar boys again, and doesn't want to, and would we like some chips? Ta, we say, great; it'll be hours before Dai's cooked the tup, if he ever stops bellyaching and gets on with it. We eat the chips in the front room where we can keep an eye on the track outside. Lizzie guesses why we're watching out and says what we do is our own business, but she doesn't want Jaz getting into no more fights. She looks fierce when she says it, and I think it can't be much fun watching your son get beat up on your own doorstep. Wayne says we're maybe saving Jaz a fight, if the boys are still after the Guzzi, and Lizzie mutters that no bike's worth getting hurt for and she wishes Jaz had just given it to them. She doesn't mean it though.

We wait an hour or so, and then Mitch says we ought to get back to Dai's to make sure he's got the lamb rigged up proper. As we leave Wayne gives Lizzie a squeeze, making her go pink and call him a wicked boy, and we tell her to lock up tight and not to expect Jaz back, because the barbecue'll go on all night.

As soon as we turn into Dai's field we know something's wrong. The fire's not even lit, Pete and Dai are shouting at each other in front of the bus, Karin's screaming at Pete, and Jaz's sitting next to Josie on the back step with his boots off and his head in his hands like he just died.

Josie comes running over. 'They got the Guzzi! Just walked down while Jaz was asleep and we didn't know who they were.'

'Fucking left the key in it, didn't I,' wails Jaz. 'Drove it straight off.'

'Just as well,' Karin snaps, coming up. 'Carrying lump hammers, they were. Saw them.'

'Then why didn't you say so?' yells Pete. 'Stupid cow.'

'Thought they were a couple of Dai's mates, shithead,' Karin shouts back. 'There's always blokes in and out of here.' She's steaming with rage.

'What I want to know,' says Dai, scratching his beard and looking bewildered, 'is how they knew to come here?'

Nobody bothers to answer him, it's such a stupid question. Jaz's got the only big Guzzi in town, and everyone knows he knows Dai, and where the bus is parked. I'm thinking about what's strapped to the back of the Guzzi. No sign of a feed bag on the grass. Can't decide if it complicates things or not.

'We'll go get it back,' says Mitch, wheeling his bike round.

'I'm coming,' says Jaz, struggling to get his boots on.

Wayne gives him his helmet back and gets a spare from the bus. I remember what Lizzie said about Jaz staying out of fights, but I reckon it's his bike and if there's four of us no one should get hurt. Wayne gets on behind me, Jaz behind Mitch. I tell Wayne about the feed bag as we bump up the field and he says, 'Uhuh,' like he's got to ponder it too.

We go to Tredegar first, the back mountain way. The way you'd go if you'd nicked a big spiteful bike and needed some easy miles to get used to it. Then up into town, round the clock tower, and cruise the streets a while. See a couple of kids on Yams and ask them if they've seen a big Guzzi with two up, but they say they haven't.

We stop in a lay-by the north end of town to decide where to go next. Jaz nods towards the Heads of the Valleys road up ahead and says they'll go for a thrash, definite, they won't be able to resist it. 'Bet they total it,' he moans.

'Which way d'you reckon?' I say. 'Merthyr or Aber?'

'Merthyr,' says Wayne. Jaz and Mitch nod. Aber way the boys'd be heading back on themselves.

We eat up the miles for five minutes or so. Big bare road, the Heads, flattened spoil heaps either side, no trees, no hedges to hide behind. Then, up at Dowlais Top, just before the road sweeps wide of Merthyr, we get lucky. There's a garage at the roundabout and on the forecourt there it is, the Guzzi, and beside it, two lads in helmets. But it's not as lucky as it could be, because parked in front of the Guzzi there's a cop car, and standing by the lads, two flat-top coppers. And shit, the feed bag's still strapped to the Guzzi.

We slow right down to enter the forecourt and park the bikes a distance away. The cops have seen us and we don't want them nervous, so after we've propped the bikes we take our helmets off. I lay a hand on Jaz, to stop him rushing over and saying too much. If the cops know the Guzzi's stolen, and the boys tell him why, it could be in a lock-up for months while they argue about it.

Wayne's thinking the same; as we walk over he hisses, 'Don't mouth off about nothing, right?'

The cops wave us to a halt a few yards from the boys. They don't want us mixing with them till they've sussed us out. I'm trying to see what the lads look like under their helmets, in case we need to find them later.

'What d'you boys want?' one of the coppers asks. He's a big red-haired fella. I recognise him, we've met him before.

'That bike's a friend of ours,' says Wayne, smiling at him easy. 'Just come to see how it's doing.'

The copper stares at us. Not unfriendly-like, just letting his mind tick. I look past him to the feed bag. Feet and head and guts . . . it's been a hot day . . .

The copper's eyes settle on Jaz. A moment registering the bruises. Then, 'You,' he says. 'You're Jason Williams, aren't you?'

'Yep,' agrees Jaz.

'This your bike?' He gestures towards the Guzzi.

'Yep,' says Jaz.

'You give these boys permission to ride it?'

Jaz takes a while to think about this. Then shrugs. 'Maybe.'

'That's what they say. That you said they could take it.'

'We said a spin,' I say quickly, before Jaz can foul things up. 'Not all day.'

'So you want it back, right?' The copper's voice says he doesn't believe us, he knows it's nicked, but he's not going to push it.

'Yeah,' says Jaz, after catching my eye. 'May as well.'

'OK,' says the copper, stepping back. 'You take it across to the others. Then you lads go home, right? That's that-away.' He points back the way we've come.

We all smile and say, 'Sure,' and 'Right,' like we're not going to cause him any trouble. As Jaz walks over to the Guzzi I call out, 'Give the boys their bag. They'll be wanting that.'

It takes a second for the Tredegar boys to grasp what we're talking about. Then they glance at each other quick. They don't know how to play it. Hope they're as stupid as they look. Jaz unstraps the feed sack from the grab bar.

'Shit,' he says, acting indignant as he lifts it off. 'You've scratched the paintwork, what d'you want to tie this on here for?'

The red-haired copper narrows his eyes at the lads. He's picked up their confusion, but hasn't read it right. 'What you got in there, boys?' he asks.

Jaz drops the bag on to the concrete. It hits the ground with an interesting squelch.

'It's not ours,' one of the lads says, but it comes out rushed, and even I don't believe him. Jaz says, 'Well, it weren't here this morning,' as if it's nothing to him, and dusts his hands off.

As the red-haired copper squats down to the bag his mate stabs a finger at Jaz. 'Now hoppit,' he says.

We don't need telling twice. Reckon we've got about five seconds. We race over to the bikes and start them up quick, to drown out any shouts, and don't look round as we fasten our helmets. Just a peek back as we roar out of the forecourt. The bag's standing upright and open on the concrete. One of the lads has got a hand to his belly, the other's turned away, pinching his nose. The red-haired copper's on walkabout, arm across his mouth. Wish I had a camera.

We have to take it easy back to field, we're laughing so much. Wayne keeps hitting my shoulder with his helmet. 'Oh shit,' he keeps gasping, almost knocking me off the bike. Jaz is arsing around on the Guzzi, circling all the roundabouts twice, punching the sky like he's taking victory laps. Mitch sheepdogs us at the rear, lights blazing, grinning all over his face.

And when we get back, the bonfire's lit, and Pete's got the tup spitted above it. We can smell roast lamb from the top of the field. Everyone jumps up as they see the Guzzi and suddenly it's a celebration, not a wake. The start of a magic night: stories to tell, evidence to eat, cops to watch out for, and scores even. Best barbecue for years.

THE PURSUIT OF BEAUTY

This was the third afternoon Mark had followed the girl to the gallery.

The first time she'd swung into the dark entrance, the day before yesterday, he'd almost groaned with disappointment. Just yards from the tourist crowds of Trafalgar Square; there was bound to be a huge entrance fee. But then, sidling closer, he had scanned the frontage below the words 'National Portrait Gallery', stepped a tentative foot through the glass doors, and discovered it was free. Free! She couldn't have made it easier.

She hadn't gone up the wide foyer steps into the main first floor rooms of the gallery but had hurried left, following signs that said 'Toilets' and – it was only on the second afternoon the words registered – 'The Pursuit of Beauty'. Very funny. Ha ha. A narrow stairway led down to a small basement exhibition – just one room, but partitioned into sections – on the theme of Beauty, displaying clothes, wigs, body adornments, make-up. There was even an area with a curtained-off cubicle where visitors could try on exhibits – corsets and wigs, mostly – gaze at themselves in mirrors, and take photos of each other. Not that the girl did. She simply removed pen and pad from her patchwork suede rucksack, and then either stared at the exhibits, or wrote. A college project, it had to be.

The girl's name was Patsy. Mark knew this because he had heard her friends call her that. These were the friends she met at lunch time, who would be already seated at one of the tables in the college Buttery, and who always called out to her while she was at the counter. *Hi, we're over here, Patsy! Over here!* Patsy. Not actually, he thought, a very beautiful name.

He leafed through the free, shiny-blue exhibition brochure, aware of Patsy getting out her notebook, a curve of pink tongue flicking over her strong white teeth. The brochure asked visitors to consider the notion of 'beauty'; the role of fashion, advances in health and hygiene, the desire to flaunt wealth. Whether there were immutable criteria, or whether, as the saying went, it was all in the eye of the beholder. By 'beauty' they meant personal beauty. Not landscapes, sunsets. They meant sexual attractiveness. In Mark's opinion, the beholder was king. Patsy was beautiful. Beautiful, that is, if the word described a quality that drew your gaze and held it, stirred your mind and body. Patsy was his kind of beautiful. A big girl. Not fat. Not at all. But athletically, strongly built. Clear, determined eyes. A natural, unblemished complexion. Thick no-nonsense hair, dark and short. Like a sportswoman. A swimmer. Or a runner. He loved the utilitarian look, the muscular *unfleshiness* of the bodies of sportswomen.

Why did you like one thing, and not another? It was a mystery. But a fixed mystery. Immutable, within. What you liked, you liked. It wasn't a choice. And Patsy was beautiful to him, even now.

If he had not thought her beautiful, he would never have approached her. And if he'd never approached her, she wouldn't have had the chance to humiliate him.

He twisted the brochure in his hands. Oh, self-pity was a contemptible emotion. Last night, in his hutch-like room at the hostel, with its scratched and scribbled walls –

suggesting its previous inhabitants had been unwilling inmates, rather than merely unsettled, unsupported young men – he had given himself a talking-to. Reminded himself why he had got a job at the college. After all, you could clear tables, stack washing machines, mop greasy floors, anywhere. London was full of kitchens. He'd taken the job because it was in a college, where he would be surrounded by young people like himself. Well, maybe not *like* himself, but at least *young* like himself. All shapes and sizes. She couldn't be the only beautiful one. So why allow himself to become so obsessed with her? Why be so disappointed? Stupid. There had to be others.

But the talking-to hadn't worked. Patsy and her friends were not like him. Patsy herself had reminded him of this, in those few hurtful seconds. Made it plain that he was as different from her as, say, a worm is from a butterfly. Unconnected beings. Butterflies were bright, sociable, fresh-air creatures, nurtured on the sweet, wholesome, juices of flowers. Oblivious of the worms below, toiling alone in the cold soil, forced, just to survive, to ingest the muck and mess of the earth.

She had no idea how long he had waited to catch her on her own, how much courage it had taken to walk over to the table where she was sitting, collect plates, disgusting with cigarette butts, slops of coffee. Perhaps she wouldn't have cared, if she had known. She had no conception of the effort it had taken him to smile and say the words, 'Hi, just made it again today, then?' She was always late at the Buttery, always one of the last to be served. Her reaction was as if somewhere miles away an insignificant but irritating bell had sounded, momentarily distracting her. She hadn't even looked at him. Just issued a weary under-breath, 'What's it to you?' picked up her bulging rucksack, and stalked away.

What had it been to him? A lot. More than a tremor of interest, a small lungful of air. Much more. A fortnight of anticipation. A fortnight of girding-up. A fortnight of hopes, imaginings. She looked so right. She was right. Yet she thought him undeserving of the merest touch from her eyes. Just marched away.

He lifted his own eyes from the catalogue to one of the gallery mirrors and studied himself. He did it every time, he did it now. That was what the mirrors were for. Was there something wrong with him? Well, yes, obviously. Inside. Some flaw, some deficiency, that, since he had become aware of it – recognized it – had relegated him to wormdom. But did it show? He frowned at himself. Below the brown skullcap of cropped hair resentful brows burred together. Dog-like. He relaxed them. Better. His white T-shirt was clean, neat. He wasn't ugly. He might be inside, but not on the surface. He looked normal, he was sure. Unnoticeable, of course, as worms were – even this third afternoon he seemed quite invisible to Patsy – but ordinary.

He dropped his gaze quickly; a member of the gallery staff had appeared behind him, the same uniformed man who had been here yesterday, and the day before. Mark stared down blindly at the catalogue in his hand. He should have brought a notepad with him, pretended he was a student like Patsy. The man was bareheaded, with keys and radio at his waist. Security guard uniform. Middle thirties, bulky in his thick jacket – it was cool down here, the air-conditioning ferocious – perhaps ex-services. It was his job, presumably, to notice people, and what they were doing. Shit, shit.

Yesterday, he recalled, the man had hung around nearby too. It was a small area; all the same, the mirrors had nearly always contained some part of him. A segment of powerful shoulder, a broad swathe of felted back, a strong, watchful profile. Mark had been as aware of him as of Patsy. He had felt cockier yesterday, though; even considered giving him a smile. Brazening it out. You clock me, I clock you, what of it? He'd done nothing wrong. He didn't mean any harm. Certainly not to Patsy. He wasn't a psycho. He'd curved his lips in preparation but, at the last minute, lost his nerve.

Today, in the mirror at least, the man appeared to be grinning directly at him. Sharp blue eyes. A challenging grin. It said, I know you're up to something.

But he wasn't, was he? Not really. Not *actively*. Perhaps the man knew more than he did? The future, to himself, was a blank. The day before yesterday he had given up on Patsy as she left the building. She'd stopped dead on the pavement to look at her watch, and he'd almost stepped on her heel. He'd panicked. Swung about and walked swiftly away, without looking back. Yesterday he'd followed her as far as the tube station but he didn't know where she was bound so it was pointless going further. Anyway, he had to get back to the college before the Buttery re-opened at four. Her journey had to be routine, though, because she didn't stop at the machines or the window. She must have had a return, or a season ticket. Today he had already bought his own ticket. The investment of a few pounds, giving him the freedom to travel anywhere on the Underground. And he had got someone to cover for him at the college. Having bought the ticket, he would have to use it. So a future, of some sort, stretched ahead.

He had dreamed the perfect future, of course. The culmination, anyway. Never mind how, exactly, this future started. He and Patsy walked together through the London streets, hand in hand. It was dark. Always dark. Her grip was fierce. The world was a pleasure-garden of crisp bright lights and velvety, inviting shadows. She had chosen him.

He was hers. Unconditionally. When they were passing one of the shadows, the most velvety and inviting, she fixed him with bold eyes and led him in. There, invisible in the blackness, she pushed her strong body against his, held him with such force he could hardly breathe. She wanted him as much as he wanted her. No, more. He need do nothing except acquiesce. She was experienced, built for control. It was she who bruised her lips on his, she who wrenched at their clothes, she who breathed urgency in his face. She who, eventually, pushed herself on to him.

That Patsy, ah, she understood. She knew. She accepted how he was. No, more; she desired him like that. They matched, perfectly. He had no reason to feel deficient. No reason to feel shame. He was what she wanted. She made it all so simple. How could he let that go? He'd seen the strength in her. Fantasies were forever, and the girl in them, once vague, now wore her face. She was meant for him. She just didn't know it.

The museum guard couldn't see inside his head. And so what if he could? There was no law against fantasies. No law against being in the same place as the object of those fantasies. Imaginings weren't acts. His imaginings couldn't become acts, anyway, without Patsy's cooperation. Obviously. Without that, *nothing* could happen.

He'd moved aside from the mirror and realized he was staring at an exhibit. A headless, handless dummy, like a tailor's dummy, dressed in fashionable male attire of the Elizabethan period. In those days, apparently, an artificial paunch was in favour, called a peascod. So named, the brochure said – he'd read it now a dozen times – because it resembled the shape of a pea pod. He couldn't see this, but that's what it said. The front of the peascod dipped to a point below the stomach bulge, drawing attention to the much smaller padded lump below, the codpiece covering the genitals, stuffed so as to make the penis appear erect. Elizabethans, it said in the catalogue, considered an appearance of permanent arousal virile. The effect, Mark thought, on a handless, decapitated body, was grotesque.

He heard a chuckle behind him. He felt himself flush. The guard was laughing. At him? For standing, gazing at this? Was he somehow betraying himself? To check he would have to swing round, but he couldn't do it. There were other people close by, the murmur of voices; the guard might be laughing at anything.

Patsy was less than ten feet away, the other side of the partition to his right. If he leant forward he could just see her back, over one shoulder the patchwork rucksack. She was interested in wigs today. Ludicrous, metre-high wigs. The brochure said they had been greased with lard, which attracted mice and insects. What was she doing? Sketching? Beyond her cameras flashed. Foreign-sounding giggles erupted from the alcove where visitors could play at dressing-up. Patsy had never been tempted. Well, you needed a friend with you to take the pictures. To lace the corsets, arrange the wigs. Patsy had always come alone.

He'd been here now nearly an hour. She would leave soon. On both previous days she had left before half three. Perhaps she lived out of London – lots of students did – and wanted to start her return journey before the rush hour.

Perhaps she lived somewhere with trees, and lanes, and quiet places, even if they weren't dark. Perhaps, away from her friends, her student life, she would notice him. Recognize who – what – he was. And reveal herself. Discover her power—

The girl turned abruptly, and her eyes passed over him. He held his breath. If her eyes stopped, if she registered anything, surprise, curiosity, even alarm, he would smile at her. He was melting. Not alarm, he hoped. No, not from Patsy.

But her eyes registered nothing. He was nobody. The sensation was like a cruel fist pressed against his heart. What was he doing here? Pursuing pain? This was idiotic, masochistic. And yet . . . Patsy was packing the notebook away now, moving slowly, restrapping the rucksack, towards the exit stairs. He thrust the sense of futility away. What else was there? Who else was there? He had to follow.

But he'd give her a moment. He knew where she was going so it would be easy to catch her up outside. After tucking the brochure back into the rack he ambled, glancing left and right at exhibits, towards the stairs. Touched his shirt pocket, checking the Underground ticket was still there.

As he put a foot on the bottom step a male voice behind him said quietly, 'Wait there now, laddie.'

The accent was strongly Scottish. Was someone talking to him? He swung round.

The security guard came alongside. Crooked a finger at him and murmured, 'Come with me a wee minute.'

'What?' He blinked into the man's face. It wore a stern-fatherly expression that didn't match its age.

'Just a wee minute.' The man laid a firm hand on Mark's forearm, pushing him on up the steps.

Mark tried to make his own expression outraged. The man must have realized he was following Patsy. Or did he think he had stolen something? A hand had been laid on him once leaving Top Man, when he had been stealing; that occasion had earned him, as the notices on the wall promised, a ride in a police car. He didn't want an argument here. He had to catch Patsy up. He couldn't lose her, not today. At least the man was steering him up the stairs, in the right direction.

At the half landing the man pushed at a door in the side wall marked 'Staff Only' and tried to steer him through. Mark resisted. The man chuckled, a dizzying sound, and said, 'Come on, laddie.' He tugged at him gently.

Either he made a scene, drew embarrassing attention to himself, or he followed the man inside. What choice did he have? If he was made to turn out his pockets it would be over quickly, since the man would find nothing of interest. The room was a cramped office: two chairs, a desk, telephone, the far wall obscured by filing cabinets and cardboard boxes, some of them open. He recognized the blue contents. Catalogues. The guard closed the door behind them.

'Well?' Mark demanded.

'Ah, well.' The man tipped his head. A mocking gesture.

'Why have you brought me here?'

'Och, we both know that, don't we?'

'I haven't done anything wrong.'

'No indeed.' The man's tone was strongly amused. 'Nothing wrong at all.'

'So? So?'

The guard prodded him gently in the chest with his fingertips. Mark stepped back, alarmed.

'I've had my eye on you, laddie.'

'I told you, I've—'

'And you've had your eye on me, haven't you?'

'What?'

'Come on, boy, I've seen you. Yesterday, and the day before. Can't stay away, can we?'

Mark shook his head urgently. Oh shit, he thought. Shit. But what could he say? *No no, you've made a mistake. I've been following a girl . . .*

'Fiddling around. Waiting. Dreaming.'

'Please, I've got to go.' Patsy would be crossing Trafalgar Square, striding further away—

'Mischievous dreams. I've seen them.' He touched the corner of his eye. 'Very mischievous dreams.'

'No, you've got it wrong. I'm sorry—'

'Oh, don't you worry now.' The man's blue eyes twinkled, as if he was about to impart good news. 'No call for apologies. I'm not complaining. Been dreaming a little mischief too.'

The man's nearness was overpowering. The uniform, the knowing, smiling face. His bulk filled the world. Mark couldn't think. Patsy was a tiny dot somewhere at the edge of the universe. A tiny, receding, vanishing dot.

'Come on, laddie, don't be a tease on me.'

'I don't know what you mean—'

The man heard the lie in his voice. He laughed and as if it was the most normal, natural thing in the world, started to unbuckle his trouser belt. Mark watched him, frozen with disbelief.

'Prefer dreaming, eh? That's it, is it? Ah . . .' The man sighed fondly. 'Be brave, pretty boy. I'll show you better than dreaming.'

He took out his cock and rested it on his palm. Mark stared down at it. I'm going to faint, he thought. Jesus Christ. The blind eye of the tip lifted, as if searching for something.

'See, nothing to it, and here it is noddin' and smilin' at you. Put your hand on it, laddie.'

'No, Jeez—' Mark backed away, but found himself against the wall. I'm definitely going to pass out, he thought.

'Och, come on laddie.' Impatiently the guard grasped Mark's hand and folded it round his cock. Mark watched him do it. His hand had lost volition. A dead, helpless limb. Is this terror? he thought. Why can't I pull away? He felt ridges either side of the fleshy hardness, like ivy tendrils welded to warm stone.

'Nothing to be shy of, bonny boy.' The man exhaled

contentedly. His eyelids flickered, as if he was drifting away. He recovered himself. 'Now, let's be having you.'

'No,' whispered Mark. 'Please. No.'

'Don't be silly, lad.' Careful not to disturb the hand on his cock, he undid Mark's fly buttons. I am so frightened, Mark thought, that I am paralysed. That must be it. I'm so frightened, it's beyond feeling. There's nothing I can do.

'Lovely boy,' the man murmured, reaching in and fondling him. 'Aah, aah.' He rocked his hips slowly. 'Now, isn't that grand? Isn't that friendly? Looking after each other. Nothing more to it.'

Mark closed his eyes. In a moment this would stop. It would all be over. The man's cock seemed to have ribs in it, he could feel them under the skin. He was trembling so violently he wasn't sure who was moving.

The man was murmuring endearments, like reciting a mantra. 'Darlin' laddie, such a pretty one, oh, what a pretty one, oh what a beauty . . .'

Mark's eyes watered. A joke. An appalling joke.

The cock jerked in his hand. Pulsed once, twice, thrice. The ribs melted. Mark dropped his hand. Sticky. Oh God. But the fingers on his own genitals had rested. Was that it? Was it over? Some of the eye-water spilt over his lower lids.

There was a moment of stillness before the man cleared his throat and whispered, 'Ah, don't cry, laddie.' His face moved very close, his breath hot in Mark's ear. 'Nothing here to make you cry.'

How could he say that?

'I'm not forgetting you,' the man murmured. 'Don't worry now. Just a moment. A bit shy, is it? Such a pretty dick, it won't leave with nothing. Wouldn't be fair, would it?'

Mark started to shake his head, but stopped himself. What was the right answer?

The man hesitated, as if he was thinking, and then tightened his grip. 'A little rougher for you, laddie? Is that your way? No shame in it, no shame at all. We like what we like, don't we?' He moved his hand more vigorously. 'There, need to be pushed a bit, do we, no pain no gain, that's what they say. Oh, there's lots like a bit of forcing, relieves the mind, I daresay.'

Mark wanted to wail stop, please, I'm not like you, I'm not that desperate, I'm not that lonely. I don't like this. Except his body, his traitorous body, didn't agree. It was responding. It was turning the man's bulk, against his will, into a huge dark haven. The grip on his penis had become something detached, unstoppable, irresistible. The protestations in his head were reduced to sparks, smothered by a rolling force. Ten times, a thousand times Patsy. Rougher and rougher, harder and harder, pumping sensation into him.

The force was speaking. 'That's it,' he heard it say. 'See, it knows what it likes. Coming to join us. That's it, that's it.'

Somehow his forehead had found the man's shoulder. A felty wool. Solid and unyielding. He pushed against it. It was going to happen. It had to happen. Now. Now. Oh, the shame. Oh God. Oh God.

The hand on his cock loosened, slid away from him. Mark trembled against the man's shoulder. He felt suddenly unsupported. Back from a world in which, for a few moments, he had lost himself. Been forced to lose himself. He didn't want to be back. He couldn't bring himself to pull away, because he would have to look into the man's face.

The nape of his neck was being stroked. He blotted his eyelashes on the thick wool.

'Now, now,' the man murmured.

I have just been assaulted, Mark told himself. A double

assault. First compelled to give pleasure, and then to receive it. I couldn't stop it. It wasn't my fault.

'That's what you wanted, isn't it?' He was being gently pushed away. From the angle of the man's head he knew he was being studied. He kept his eyes lowered.

'Make yourself tidy now.' The man pushed a paper towel into his hand. Then stepped back and did up his trousers. 'And I'll brew us a spot of tea.'

'No,' Mark mumbled. He scrunched the towel up in his palms. 'I have to go.' His face, he knew, was flaming.

'Oh, but you're a funny one.' The man laughed quietly and drew him towards one of the chairs. 'Now don't run away. Just a bit of loving, we all need that, laddie. A little loving and nice cup of tea. What could be better?'

Mark steadied himself on the chair back, staring down at the wooden seat. His legs were shaking. He remembered his trousers and fumbled the fly closed. 'Please. Can I go now?'

The man shrugged. 'You do as you like, bonny boy. No one's stopping you.'

Patsy would be long gone. He would never catch her now. His mind sagged. Oh Patsy, Patsy.

'Sit down, won't you?' suggested the guard.

Mark shook his head.

'Och, stop havering.' The man plucked impatiently at his sleeve. 'Sit.'

Mark hesitated, then gave up. Nothing worse could happen. He had nothing else to do. He sat.

The man chuckled and patted his shoulder. 'There now, I'm getting you, aren't I? What a performance. Well, well.'

Mark watched him plug the kettle in, drop teabags into a small enamel teapot. He heard the words again.

'What d'you mean?' he asked. What performance? And how was the man 'getting' him?

'Och, we're all different. Nothing wrong in that.' The man filled the pot with boiling water, stirred it.

Mark stared at the teapot. He didn't understand. He watched a thin thread of steam issuing from the spout.

The man poured the teas, then sat down and stretched out his legs, resting them on one of the unopened boxes. Mark picked up his mug and sipped it.

The man was smiling to himself. 'You'll come back tomorrow,' he said.

Mark put the mug down. What? Disbelievingly he said, 'I don't think—'

'You're not listening, laddie.' The man's smile had become wider. Provocative. 'I wasn't askin'. I was tellin' you. You come back tomorrow.'

Something inside Mark shook. The man glanced at him, then tipped his head to the ceiling. He was grinning, delighted with himself.

Mark's mind whirled. Why was the man looking like that? As if he had just performed an experiment and got the result he expected? What had he done? Nothing. He forced himself to speak. He had to explain.

'I was here,' he said jerkily, 'hoping a girl—'

'Och no.' The man exploded into a barking laugh. 'No no, laddie.'

'What? What's funny? I'm telling you. A girl—'

'No no. You're mistaken, laddie. Dear me. Lasses don't play your games. No no.'

What games? What was he talking about?

'You don't want a girlie, laddie. Not for what you want. Och, don't torture yourself.'

What was the guard saying? That he didn't know his own desires?

'Where's the beauty in it, laddie?' The man's voice had become comfortable. 'That's what you have to ask yourself. The real beauty. That's the question.'

Mark stared at him. He was talking in riddles.

'You think on that,' the man sighed.

'I don't understand,' said Mark flatly. 'I don't know what you're talking about.'

'Och, course you do. It's the same for everyone. Different, mind, but the same.' He tapped his temple. 'The picture. Up here. What we're looking for. The real beauty. And didn't you just have it, laddie? Didn't I give it to you?'

No, said Mark fiercely to himself, you didn't. You assaulted me. You frightened me. And yet, here he was, sitting freely beside the man. Just because the man had asked him to. Told him to. He tried to imagine what had happened earlier without the shock, without the fear.

'No,' he said, shaking his head vehemently. 'No.'

The man lowered his feet, swung more upright in his chair. A look of friendly exasperation on his face. 'Come here,' he said.

Mark frowned at him.

The man tapped the arm of his chair. 'Here.' He beckoned impatiently.

Mark found himself rising.

'That's right. Good boy. Stand there. Now. What's your name, laddie?'

'Mark.'

'Mark. That's a nice name. Well, you're with Rob, Mark. Now. Close your eyes.'

'Why?'

'I'm going to teach you something.'

'Teach me what?'

'Och, you'll exhaust a man. Close them.'

Mark closed his eyes. He sensed the man shift position, and then felt his right thigh encased in two strong hands. The muscles of his leg tensed. Then relaxed, a little. He could always shake the hands off.

'Now,' said the man's voice. 'I've got you, haven't I?'

Mark waited.

'Answer me.'

Mark cleared his throat. 'Yeah.'

'And—' the hands moved up his thigh. Big, powerful hands, stroking, squeezing him, '—I could be all over you, couldn't I, laddie?'

Mark pressed his eyelids tight.

'Touching you, loving you. Couldn't I?'

The man waited. Mark gave a tiny nod.

'Come on, I want to hear you.' He felt himself squeezed, urged.

'Yes.'

'And you wouldn't stop me, would you? Wouldn't lift a finger.'

What was this teaching him? The meaning of shame? Humiliation?

'I might,' he whispered. 'I could.'

'Aye, but you won't.'

The man was ripping him open. The worm was struggling, trying to bury itself deeper.

'Because you don't want to.'

Silence.

'Mark?'

There was nowhere to go. Nowhere to hide.

'Say it,' the man murmured.

'I can't.'

'You can.'

'No—'

'Yes. Be brave, laddie.'

Mark inhaled. Just enough to whisper, 'I wouldn't stop you.'

'There you are.' The hands gripped and shook him in congratulation. 'Not so hard, was it? That's your beauty, laddie. That's what you're looking for.'

Mark still had his eyes closed. The blackness in front of him swam. He imagined trying to pull away now, and, yes, being tugged back. Pulling away harder, being held harder. The powerful, inexhaustible grip of the man. The moment of exquisite capitulation. Shit, he was getting a hard-on. He opened his eyes, alarmed.

Rob was grinning up at him. 'See? Got you going, didn't I? And you won't get that from a lassie, now, will you?' He squeezed his hands so fiercely Mark gasped. 'Nor from anything in there.' He jerked his head contemptuously at the door. He meant the exhibition. 'It's inside you, laddie. That's where your beauty is. Waiting, shining for you. Just need someone to get you there. Och, it's not so rare. It takes all sorts.'

There was nothing judgemental in his face. Is he saying it's normal? Mark thought. It can't be. I know it isn't.

'You want to be careful, though, laddie. It's a risky game.'

I didn't choose it, Mark thought.

'But no danger here, laddie. None at all. I'll give you your beauty.' He pushed Mark away with a chuckle, flicked his fly. 'An' no need for long faces. Or is that how you like it, laddie? A martyr boy, are you?' He waved a hand, smiling, dismissive. 'Go on with you. Off after your day. You just come back tomorrow, eh, like a good boy. We'll see each other right.'

Mark stepped out from the gallery into a dazzling afternoon. The air, after the refrigerated atmosphere inside, felt stunningly hot. The sun's rays were a burning pressure on his skin. He made no decision but found himself turning right, towards the tourist hubbub of Trafalgar Square. Less than a minute's walk. From the wide pavement outside the National Gallery he looked down into the Square. The stone lions, fountains, statues, Nelson's column itself, were exotic islands in a colourful sea of T-shirts, sunhats, baseball caps, rucksacks. Cameras round every neck. People sat on the low parapets round the fountain basins, facing inwards, kicking bare feet in the clear water. Drenched children shrieked and splashed in the knee-high pools.

Slowly he descended the crowded steps to the floor of the Square. A fountain in front of him was spraying diamonds into the water.

Something terrible had happened to him, and he was in shock.

Or it hadn't, and he wasn't.

GETTING A LIFE

It was a tedious start to the July day that was to be the worst – to date – in DC Sarah Grant's twenty-five-year-old life. She was sitting in an unmarked police car at just before seven in the morning, in the car park of one of the city's shabbiest towerblocks, beside one of the least attractive male officers of her force. Even so early in the morning, and only an hour after coming on duty, the man beside her – DC Andy Gitting – smelt. The odour was of stale curry, unwashed armpits, and festering resentment. They had been parked twenty minutes, and hadn't spoken for the last ten. Gitting was sucking a throat lozenge, adding occasional fiery blasts of menthol to the fetid atmosphere, and refusing to relinquish his anger at having drawn the short straw. Twice. Not only was he partnered with a female officer – one of only two on the shift – but was separated, with her, from the real action, which was about to happen a mile away. This action was a decent, adrenalin-intoxicating early morning raid, on the overnight hideout of a bail-absconding, violent, indisputably nasty thug. And what had they got? A surprise visit to a sleepy twenty-two year old, a petty offender unlikely to offer resistance, who, after the briefs had done their work, would probably walk away with a suspended. Or nothing at all. What crime had he committed, they'd argue, except give a recent nights' houseroom to that nasty thug, a thug, moreover, whose dangerous company he was known to do his best to avoid, but who had the armtwisting clout of being his mother's ex-husband?

This was a waste of time. Moppers up, that's all they were.

Sarah broke the silence. She said, 'Mind, it'll take us a few minutes up to the eighth floor. Bet the lifts aren't working.'

'They said seven o'clock,' muttered Gitting. 'They'll get seven. Keen to see pretty boy, are we?'

Sarah sighed. Spite had put her here. Double standards. She wished she'd never opened her mouth. The men could be as crude as they liked about female suspects. But let a woman police officer make an unguarded remark about a male under surveillance, and you never heard the end of it. The remark hadn't even been crude; just an involuntary, 'Wow, bring him to my tent,' a second after she'd lifted the binoculars. Such an energetic-looking, quick-smiling young man. And not really a villain himself; well, not as criminal as he *might* have been, given his relatives. Carelessly lawless, rather than *bad*. Cheeky though. He'd grinned straight at them the next day, and raised a rude finger. At the briefing the Sergeant had said, 'And Grant can have the pleasure of getting the boy out of bed,' and the whole room had sniggered. Well, she'd smiled too. That wasn't the point. The point was that he'd then given her Gitting as partner, who was rough with victims, never mind suspects. It had to be deliberate. A move designed to punish her, at one remove, for attempting to be one of the lads.

'It's seven,' she said. Without waiting for her partner's agreement she climbed out of the car. She brushed Gitting's cigarette ash from her trousers and walked the few yards to the block entrance. Gitting was following. Inside the lobby she ignored the lifts. No evidence that they were out of order, but a balls-up of the most routine part of this morning's operation would be hard to live down. She started trudging up the concrete stairs. Gitting, a half-flight below her, was puffing loudly by the second floor. Unfit bastard. Not a soul about. Hardly surprising – no children or pensioners above the first floor in these disgraceful old blocks. A quarter of the flats unlet. As for the rest, well, no one paying their own way would choose to live here. A tower of snoring wasters.

She had to wait on the eighth-floor landing for Gitting to catch up. She was breathing hard herself but disguising it. Gitting was wheezing, muttering, 'Bastard, bastard,' to himself. She led the way down the high-sided walkway. Outside number eighty-three they stopped. Gitting took his baton out and extended it.

'You won't need that,' Sarah murmured.

Gitting ignored her and leant on the bellpush. Nothing sounded. No bell or buzzer.

Sarah opened the letterbox, rapped hard on the wood above, and shouted, 'Steven! Open up! Police!'

They waited ten seconds. Somewhere on one of the walkways below a door banged.

'He has to be here,' said Sarah.

Gitting stood back, lifted a foot, and kicked the door in. As if it were cardboard. Parts of it possibly were. Sarah pursed her lips and followed him inside.

They found Steven barely awake. Naked and blinking at them, fuddled with sleep. Sarah couldn't help but register that, even fuddled, he was an attractive sight. Perhaps more attractive now than when he was properly, cockily, awake. He had dark, Mediterranean good looks, acquired from God knows where; certainly not from his scraggy whey-faced mother, off their patch these days, but doubt-less shacked up elsewhere with some new prison-fodder manfriend. Her son, at this moment, his handsome face confused and offguard, rising from grubby sheets in this squalid, chaotic bedroom, had the look of a fallen angel.

Afterwards, the newspapers would hint that Steven was assaulted by Gitting and that Sarah was forced to intervene to protect him. It made a better story; established character, provided motivations for what followed. But in fact Gitting never touched the boy; merely snapped rough words at him, threw him his clothes, and, once he was dressed, cuffed his wrists behind his back. Sarah remained in the bedroom throughout, read him his rights, and kept her face neutral. That was the extent of her protection.

It was then they heard the noise below. The bedroom overlooked the car park where they had left the police car. The noise they heard was of a large solid object hitting sheet metal.

'Fucking aida!' swore Gitting, staring down at the bronze roof of the vehicle, which was now askew in its parking bay. A dustcart trying to make a three-point turn had rammed it. He snapped, 'Bring him down,' to Sarah and set off, furious, to protect police property.

They would say, afterwards, that he should never have left her. But Sarah thought nothing of it. A handcuffed man with no history of violence to escort downstairs. Where was the difficulty in that?

At the top of the first flight Sarah released Steven's hands from behind his back and reshackled them in front. There were sixteen half-flights of concrete steps to negotiate and though the young man was acting cool – attempted a flirty smile, even, the chancer – he was shaky from his abrupt awakening. She could see, and feel, his hands trembling. She had no conception, as she did this, that she was performing an act that would save her life; she did it purely to prevent harm to a prisoner in custody.

It was on the sixth floor that they ran into Peter Barlow. Almost literally. One moment the landing in front of them was empty, the next a massive figure, wearing a sweat shirt that strained across his ox-like, tensed-up torso, was blocking their way. Both parties froze with shock. Then Sarah recognized him – the iron-pumping, currently most wanted man in the city, the very man that, a mile away, colleagues were breaking down other doors down to apprehend – and, in the split second before realizing it would be safer to pretend she hadn't, let him know she had. It took Barlow only the same split second to see the handcuffs on Steven's wrists, and grasp that he was staring into the face of a policewoman.

Sarah said, 'Move aside, please,' but before she had finished knew she had blown it. She stepped back, tugging at Steven with one arm, reaching for her radio with the other. She never made it. A punch with the force of a hammer hit her shoulder and sent her reeling.

The next thing she was properly aware of was being flung through a doorway, into what appeared to be a flat in the process of renovation. Or dismantlement. Bare boards, some missing, ceiling panels hanging, radiators stacked against a wall, lengths of electric cable trailing.

Her radio was gone. Where, she didn't know. Its loss made her feel naked. Terrified. Steven was being flung in after her. He cried, 'Oi! Peter!' sounding alarmed himself. Barlow snarled, 'And you stay right there,' and slammed him with winding force against the wall opposite.

Sarah knew there was no reasoning with a man like Barlow. They had been warned. His aggression is chemical. Quite indiscriminate. Do not approach him alone; if, by mischance, you find him approaching you, retreat. Under no circumstances provoke him. Roused, his rage is unstoppable.

He was picking up a crowbar that was propped in one of the holes in the floor. His eyes were on her. There was no time to do anything except grab behind her for her baton. She had walked unwittingly across his path, and now, it appeared, he was going to kill her for it.

The baton was no match for the crowbar. She saw Barlow's arm and the metal lift, and the next moment her own arm was slack, the telescopic links of the baton actually fractured, the misshapen object rolling lumpily across the boards. She felt nothing, but knew her elbow too was broken. Her legs also knew this. They simply crumpled.

Then he was standing over her, raising the bar again. This was the moment she was going to die. He would hit her on the head, now she had no way of warding off the blow, her skull would shatter, and she would die. It was so unfair.

It amazed her, afterwards, that she kept her eyes open. That even as Barlow was aiming the blow, she was looking up at him. So she saw what Steven did. Saw him rush across the three yards or so between them, and hurl himself, his whole body weight, shoulder first, at Barlow's back. There was a crack and clatter as the crowbar shot out of Barlow's hand, hit the wall behind her, and fell to the floor. The weight of the huge man's body, caught off balance, sent him staggering sideways. Steven recovered more quickly from the impact and scrabbled behind her for the crowbar. Then shot back into the middle of the room, moving with the speed of the truly terrified, holding it in his shackled hands. As Barlow recovered and swung round roaring, the young man made two quick swings with the crowbar at waist height, as if preparing to launch a throwing weight at an athletics event, and then flung it at the window.

The glass shattered with a noise like an explosion. *Why didn't he keep the crowbar?* people asked afterwards. *Why, when he must have known the danger of thwarting Barlow?* But Sarah knew, even at the time, that it was the right thing to do. The only thing to do. A man who has never used a hand-weapon in anger is unlikely to produce a felling blow first time. Certainly not constrained with handcuffs. Steven would not have got a second chance. Barlow would have regained the bar, and used it on both of them. But now there was no weapon of such deadliness in the room, and Gitting – or someone else below – would know where they were, and come up to find them.

And so he did, with others, after a delay of six minutes. Six minutes in which he tried to raise Sarah on the radio, failed, peered and shouted up the stairwell, saw nothing and received no reply, called for urgent backup, and only when it arrived joined the two other male officers in pounding up the stairs.

Six minutes in which Steven was savagely punished for saving a police officer's life. Or rather, since Barlow's thought-processes didn't run to abstractions, six minutes in which the man's rage was diverted, robotically, to the object that had attacked him, blind to any practical purpose, to his relationship with that object, or to Sarah. He used his fists first to choke off the young man's desperate shouts, and drop him to the floor. Then his trainer-clad feet, moving round the frantic, scrabbling, curled-up body, kicking his legs and knees down so he could get at his abdomen and genitals. Automatic; when you fought, it was to hurt. And then his feet too, because Steven was still gasping and sobbing and crying out, against the boy's head and face and the bloody hands vainly shielding both. Kick after kick, blow after blow. Even after Steven became silent, his body unresponsive, and quite undefended. On and on, until, finally, the policemen arrived.

For the first twenty-four hours that Sarah and Steven were in hospital there was official confusion as to what, exactly, had happened. Minor injuries to arresting officers, wishful thinking, and a natural desire not to draw attention to faulty intelligence or operational mistakes, contributed to this. Without any input from the two injured witnesses – Sarah was prescribed uninterrupted sleep after the operation to set her shattered arm, and Steven was unconscious in Intensive Care – there was even a tendency to construct a scenario in which their roles were reversed. Steven's connection with Barlow suggested a deliberate leading of Sarah into danger – he would have known, certainly, of the man's presence in one of the empty flats – and it was assumed that it was Sarah, displaying the resourceful quick-thinking typical of a well-trained officer under pressure, who had broken the window and so brought assistance to them both.

Sarah, however, soon put her colleagues right. She woke from her recuperative sleep in a state of energetic panic. Suppressed euphoria supplied the energy – she was alive! alive! – but this euphoria couldn't be acknowledged while Steven's fate was unknown. Her first coherent words were, 'Where's Steven?' She was reassured that he was downstairs in Intensive Care, holding his own and in receipt of excellent medical attention, which temporarily satisfied her. But she then started to imagine that she was being lied to – as she herself had in the past lied to protect other trauma survivors – and demanded to see him. She would not rest, she insisted, she would speak to no one, until she had seen for herself.

She was taken downstairs in a wheelchair. To someone not used to the carnage that can be inflicted on the human body the sight would have been deeply distressing. Sarah, however, had seen worse. In her six years in the force she had seen a child decapitated in a car crash, a naked woman rotted by prolonged immersion in water, and the body of a teenage boy hit by a train. All very much worse. In comparison Steven, despite the physical evidence of his injuries, the gross swelling of his flesh, the splints on fingers, wrist and lower leg, the discolourations due to internal bleeding, the wires and tubes, looked almost robustly alive. He was bodily intact, and, though still unconscious, breathing without assistance. His bruised and lacerated chest rose and fell with steady, reassuring regularity. Machines blipped unfrenetically, silent screens recorded unexceptional zigzag activity. The female doctor said that had his attacker had been wearing workboots rather than trainers it would have been a grimmer story; Steven had a skull fracture and other serious injuries, but his brain, as far as they could tell, was functioning normally. His swollen eyelids had been seen to tremble. His internal bleeds had stopped, his vital signs had stabilized. 'He saved my life,' Sarah informed her. 'He must *not* die.' He wasn't going to, the doctor promised. Sarah was taken back to her room, where she cried cathartically for an hour, then called for a huge meal and wolfed it down.

Her account of the traumatic morning, when she came to give it, couldn't have been clearer. She was not interested in allocating blame or scapegoating – as far as she was concerned Gitting, for instance, had done nothing wrong, nothing she might not have done herself – or in presenting her own actions in anything but a purely factual light. Steven, she insisted, had not contrived the confrontation. Absolutely not. Indeed, what she wanted made crystal clear was that in her opinion – and it should be the opinion of any objective person – he had performed an act of astonishing bravery, from a position of relative safety, and in full awareness of the danger to himself. She, and the

police force on her behalf, should publicly acknowledge
this bravery. She suggested a press conference which,
injuries permitting, she would be happy to attend. There
they should, immediately and unreservedly, make explicit
their heartfelt gratitude to him.

At this point her colleagues and superiors decided Sarah
had gone soft. It stuck in the collective craw. There was no
way that a police force, as much as it valued its officers,
was going to express gratitude for the life of one of them to
a petty criminal. This was what Steven was. His record
showed numerous cautions and convictions for soft-drug
possession, minor car crime and opportunist theft, and
highlighted status as a 'known associate' of a dangerous
felon, to wit, Barlow. It was suggested to her, tactfully, that
Steven's actions, while on the face of it laudable, could be
viewed in an entirely self-serving light. Suppose she'd been
killed? What would his position have been then? Alone
with Barlow, his mother's ex-husband, and a dead police
officer. Might he not also have been blamed for the killing?

No, said Sarah. No no no. She had been there. There
hadn't been time for Steven to think ahead, to balance risks
and benefits to himself. His intervention had been instinctive.
She had seen his terror in the seconds after he'd barged
Barlow aside. He knew – better than most, surely – how
violent, indiscriminate, and lacking in control the man
was. He knew he was not exempt, that he was about to
pay for what he had done.

Her words were listened to but ignored. A statement was
issued to the press in which the facts, while presented
more or less truthfully, were cosmetically condensed. The
statement asserted that DC Sarah Grant, while escorting a
prisoner from his flat, had been unaccountably confronted
by a violent felon. Both DC Grant and her prisoner had
been attacked, and in the mêlée a window had been

broken, thus alerting a police colleague below. The felon had been swiftly apprehended by back-up officers, and although both Sarah and her prisoner had been seriously injured in the unprovoked attack, both, hopefully, were on their way to full recoveries. There then followed a paragraph outlining statistics on assaults suffered by police – male and female – in the course of their duty, and a single line stating that DC Grant would not be available for photographs or interviews.

Sarah was frustrated and angry that her wishes were ignored, but as a woman in her city force she was used to frustration and anger towards colleagues, and knew that bone-gnawing was futile. From her hospital bed she resolved to bide her time. Barlow had been charged and, eventually, she would have her say in court. So would Steven. The truth could wait.

The prosecution service charged Barlow with the attempted murder of Sarah, and grievous bodily harm to Steven. She had been attacked with a crowbar, he with fists and feet. The weapon and intent were more significant factors in the choice of charge than the harm achieved. A bonus was that the more serious charge related to the more reliable witness.

The case was scheduled to be heard in eight months. Barlow, in his remand cell, facing at least a four year sentence for the offence for which he had jumped bail, indicated his intention to plead not guilty to both new charges. He always denied charges, being wise to two facts: first, that in Britain admissions of guilt to lesser offences are available right up to the conclusion of a court case, and, second, that the evidence of victims of violence, especially where the victim has a family relationship with the accused, is notoriously problematic. With regard to the first, he and his solicitor were firmly of the opinion that a charge of attempted murder where the victim, Sarah, had suffered only a fractured elbow, was an outrageous scare tactic, and was very likely to be reduced. As to the second, Barlow was confident that Steven, once in a position to make up his own mind on the matter, would refuse point-blank to testify against him, so scuppering the GBH charge. To admit to anything, at least until they were in court and could gauge the strength of the opposition case, would therefore be extremely foolish.

Barlow, however, had misjudged the situation – at least regarding Steven. He'd overlooked how badly he had hurt him, and the practical – and other – consequences of this. Because Steven had suffered multiple injuries and needed a succession of treatments to repair these, he spent sixteen weeks in hospital. Sixteen weeks during which he progressed slowly from infant-like helplessness to near-independence. Sixteen weeks of immersion in an isolating, cocooning, totally protective environment. Sixteen weeks of solicitous, tactful, amnesiac fog. The immersion – and amnesia – was helped by the lack of visitors from outside. His mother, whose only significant gift to him during his lifetime had been the tenancy of their old flat two years ago, visited while he was still in Intensive Care. Steven appeared conscious but couldn't speak to her, and he looked horrible. His lips were swollen to a grotesque cartoon-like pout, and his eyes resembled Victoria plums. She knew her ex-husband had done this, and didn't want to think about it. She left in a panic, and never visited again. The hospital was five miles from Steven's old territory, and only two friends – or young men he'd thought of as friends – made the journey to see him. They came together a week after he was moved to a ward side-room. They giggled and swore when they first saw him, then avoided the subject of his injuries completely, as if they were an embarrassment, and left within twenty minutes. By the fourth week – by which time, ironically, his appearance would have deterred no one – he had no unofficial visitors at all. He was confined to his small room, surrounded and ministered to by men and women who knew exactly what had happened to him, demanded nothing from him, and behaved as if they genuinely cared about him. He felt mothered, fathered, sistered, brothered. Like a second childhood. There were no fronts to keep up, no vulnerabilities to hide – these people had seen him naked, in every sense. One night he actually caught himself fantasizing that the surgeon who was fixing his jaw, who had already saved nearly all his teeth, and was now concerned that something as trivial as his 'bite' would eventually be correct, was his real father. All he knew of this shadowy parent was that he had been an Italian called Stefano (hence his own name), an AC Milan football fan, who had shared a celebratory evening with his mother while in the city for an away international. The doctor wasn't Italian – his name was Mr Hamil – but it didn't matter. He was darkly handsome, benignly authoritative, and Steven was in his care. The man even seemed to enjoy the responsibility. Steven would have liked a father like Mr Hamil.

He didn't dwell on what Peter had done to him. Well, he didn't remember the attack itself. Of course he spoke to the police about events just before; officers visited regularly in the first month, adding more to their notes as his memory and capacity for conversation returned. But in his mind the pictures had little connection with himself. They were more like a film he had seen some time ago, in which he had played no part and certainly hadn't enjoyed watching, so that when his interviewer left the images were dismissed immediately from his mind.

The closest he came was when a female PC turned up, bringing him a second get-well card from Sarah – this time she'd actually signed it 'Sarah' above her title 'DC Grant' – and who sought from him confirmation that he was intending to testify against Barlow. She said, 'He thinks you won't, you know, he's counting on it.' Steven was puzzled and asked why, and she blinked at him and said, 'Well. He's assuming you'll be too scared. Obviously. Used to pushing people around, isn't he?' She smiled and added, 'God, you should know.'

A small edge of truth sank into him. Sarah had been the woman in the film-memory. The man in it had been Peter. Not an image of him, an obscurely-generated mental invention, but the real man. The man who for six of his teenage years had been his mother's husband. And he, Steven, the person he was now, had also been there. It had actually happened. That was how he could see the pictures, why the film was in his head. But it was still a horrible film. Especially towards the end. As he thought about it he felt a glimmer of the horror: Peter roaring at him, and a sensation inside him that he never, ever, wanted to feel again. He didn't want to feel it now. He fast-forwarded to the blank. That was how it had ended. Safely. In a blank.

He stopped thinking about it at all then, and over the next couple of weeks felt strength flood back into him. He even started to detect restlessness, as if he was growing impatient with his dependence and was ready for change. But nothing did change, and, indeed, a week on again, he had a minor relapse. He ached all over. He was fretful. One evening, embarrassingly, he even shed a few tears. He didn't know why. Just suddenly, one late afternoon, he was staring out of his window, past the flickering television picture on the sill into the leaf-scattered lawns and car park that had been his view for weeks, and was overwhelmed with grief. 'Feeling a bit low,' the ward sister called it. A nurse sat in his room that evening and told him all about her boyfriend until he fell asleep. The next day Mr Hamil visited, spent half an hour checking him over, and pronounced his physical progress perfectly satisfactory. He put the lowness down to the length of time he had been in hospital – a sort of institutional depression. He reassured Steven that he would be discharged as soon as practically possible – hopefully no longer than four, five more weeks – and told the Sister, in Steven's hearing, that it was time to get things moving outside.

From that moment the whole hospital organisation seemed mobilised to this end. Steven was visited by social workers, physiotherapists, Victim Support and benefit advice volunteers. His old high-rise flat was deemed unsuitable for him to return to, so a housing association was persuaded to allocate him a smaller but much nicer flat in a new low-rise development close to the hospital, and those possessions of his worth keeping from the old place were magically transported there. Criminal injuries forms were filled in for him, and cash benefits to which the temporarily disabled were entitled applied for. The home-help service agreed a month of support after discharge. It was as if the hospital, like a perfect parent, had recognized minor revolt in its adopted son, and, accepting his desire and readiness for independence, was making every effort to give him the best new start possible.

On the day he was discharged, a month later, he was kissed goodbye by a dozen female nurses – even some off-duty staff popped in – and handed a card with outpatient appointments listed at fortnightly intervals. He was reminded to nip up to the ward when he visited, so they could say hi to him. 'Don't be a stranger,' they said. He thanked them, feeling strange, but not at all a stranger. They were his family. A hospital volunteer drove him to his new flat. He was still wearing a tooth brace – Mr Hamil's bite-correction device – and was still physically wobbly, but, sitting in one of his old armchairs, waiting for the cup of tea the volunteer was making for him in his sparkling new kitchen, he told himself that he was mentally ready for this. Here he was, in a new unsordid flat, in a new, attractive neighbourhood, with no money worries, and in his pocket the phone numbers of people whose sole function, it seemed, was to offer him support. Even the tooth brace would be off in a month. Something huge had changed his life, entirely for the better. Thanks to the hospital and the people there, he was a new person. He felt the obligation of this. He promised himself, and them, a new start.

Sarah, meanwhile, was finding the going rougher. Almost a reverse journey. She'd been fine while she was at home convalescing. The euphoria of survival saw her through, and even irritation with her colleagues – with whom she wasn't yet having to rub shoulders – was put to one side. She returned to light duties after six weeks, but, the moment she stepped through the CID door, felt a mental blackness descend. It even seemed to affect her eyesight; that first day she was constantly turning on lights. Her colleagues were cheerfully welcoming but otherwise hopeless; no one mentioned her ordeal, or made allowances. She was clearly expected to slot back into her normal self as if nothing had happened. And yet something had happened, and was still happening. In that very first week, dog-tired at her desk, the room seemed to flicker – or maybe it was her eyelids – and for a split second she saw Barlow standing over her, his arm raised in fury. A monstrous apparition, the horror of which she felt unable to confide to anyone. Talk of her frailty would be round the station in hours.

And then at home, after those early weeks of solid, recuperative sleep, she started to dream, recurrently, about Steven. In the dream she saw him lying on the floor while Barlow – the vast malevolent shape was faceless, but it had to be him – beat him with a crowbar. His body was turning to pulp. She knew that this was her fault, and that she should be doing something, should be stopping the pulping, but she couldn't. Only watch. It was so horrific, so real and horrific, that she woke rigid and gasping. She started to fear sleep.

Being a sensible young woman, and suspecting that she needed help, she arranged to see a counsellor. Not a service counsellor, but one she found herself. She told the woman about her flashback and dreams, and confessed that recently she had found herself, even when not asleep, thinking constantly about Steven. This embarrassed her; the thoughts had become interwoven with earlier thoughts about his attractiveness, so it felt almost as if she was admitting to a juvenile crush on him. The counsellor relieved her mind by pointing out that it was perfectly natural to feel a powerful connection – even minor obsession – with someone with whom one had shared a terrible experience. Especially if pressure of unexpressed gratitude was involved. Backgrounds and factors such as physical attractiveness were irrelevant. If Steven were fifty, ugly and bald, she would probably feel just the same. He was simply the only person who could truly understand what she had been through, and also the very special person who – for whatever motive, it mattered not a jot – had saved her life. Not only were thoughts about him natural, but it might even be therapeutic to allow them a little rein. She understood that Sarah couldn't visit Steven at present (her superiors insisted that Barlow be given no pretext for claiming witness collusion) but she encouraged her to seek reassurance about his progress. Why not? It might at least give her more cheerful thoughts to dwell on.

So Sarah wrote Steven a second get-well card – he'd have been too ill to read the first, she told herself – and asked a female colleague, who had to visit him anyway, to take it with her. The colleague reported back that Steven had a way to go, healthwise, but that he had seemed OK. Quite unfazed about the prospect of testifying against Barlow. Remarkably unfazed. She'd only seen him a couple of times before the attack, but didn't think he looked much different. Thinner and paler and, oh yes, he was wearing a tooth brace, but otherwise, well, if you liked that sort of thing – a grin here – you'd probably still like it. Amazing what hospitals could do.

Despite irritation at the grin – how crass could colleagues get? – this did help Sarah. It allowed her to put her obsession on hold. Steven hadn't evaporated. He was still here, recovering his health, and intending to testify in court. She would see him again, and she would get her chance to express her feelings towards him – feelings that arose purely from shared experience and gratitude, she now saw.

But from then on her police work became harder. For some reason – perhaps the counselling released them – her critical faculties became more acute. And tolerance with her CID colleagues diminished. She felt herself surrounded by insensitive, thoughtless, emotionally illiterate clods. Men – and even some women – who swanned around their patches like petty overlords, bullying suspects, laughing at their misfortunes, contemptuous and disbelieving of everyone, completely blind to their own unpleasantness, and the counter-productive effects of what they were doing. To think that once, naive idealist that she must have been, she had thought police work was about doing good. A lumpen, brutalizing force. No wonder they were called pigs.

She expressed this to her counsellor, who listened sympathetically, and then asked her to consider – merely consider – whether her feelings might not be an overreaction, perhaps not unrelated to the sense of isolation and frustration that she was feeling. Limbo times could be very difficult. Sarah said rubbish, and that as soon as the court case was over she was going to resign. She'd do it before, except that she didn't want back-stabbing police machinations to spoil her day in court. The counsellor nodded and murmured that she was glad, anyway, that Sarah wasn't rushing into anything. Sarah went home, refused to think about what the counsellor had said, but found herself awash with tears anyway. She wasn't happy. She *was* isolated, she *was* frustrated. Something terrible had happened to her, which only Steven could understand. She needed to see him. She needed to talk to him. But there were still two months to go. It seemed so long. So long.

The case came to the city's Crown Court in March. The attempted murder and GBH charges were, of course, being heard together.

On the first day that Sarah and Steven were required to attend, only the usual local press court reporters were in attendance, plus one female journalist from the *Independent*, who was researching sexism in police forces, and who had a special interest in the linked (in her view) physical vulnerability, out on the street, of female officers. She had logged the brief statement issued by the city force eight months ago, and noted that the DC had been alone at the time of her attack. She was here to fill in details.

She listened with increasing interest to the prosecution

outlining the bare bones of its case – bones that were, however, vastly more meat-laden than as outlined on paper in her briefcase – and, during the lunch recess, hung about in the corridor to catch sight of witnesses being escorted to the cafeteria. She got a local contact to point Sarah and Steven out. The woman police officer looked under strain, tight-lipped and frowning. The young man Steven, however, the DC's erstwhile prisoner, dark and doe-eyed, was a dish. And this was the young man who very possibly – extrapolating facts she had just heard – had saved the young woman's life. She immediately rang for a photographer. This could make a story.

The following morning the *Independent* ran a short article, quoting brief extracts from the prosecution outline (comment would have to wait for the conclusion of the case) but accompanied by a large photograph of Steven, taken as he was leaving the court building. He was alone, hesitating on the steps, hands in his jacket pockets, shoulders hunched against the icy March wind. A few yards away was a huddle of police officers. These officers had in fact no connection with the case against Barlow, and were conscious of giving offence to no one by laughing and joking amongst themselves. The effect, however, was of lonely freeze-out on Steven's part, and a churlish back-turning on the police's. Steven also looked exceptionally handsome. More handsome, even, than he did in real life. The picture editor had deliberately selected the most appealing shot of him (as she had been asked to) but in truth had had an excess of riches to choose from. The camera simply adored the boy.

Within hours of the paper hitting the news stands, a battalion of photographers and journalists had descended on the court building. The regional press were attracted by the fact that a court case in their area had gained national attention. The national press, however, had grasped immediately the message implicit in the *Independent's* photo, and scented scandal. Possibly a cover-up, at least shameful police reticence. Plus – a crucial factor for the tabloids – the case appeared to involve a young, intensely photogenic, unsung hero. Many missed the morning court session, when the defence case was outlined, but all were present for the afternoon. This was when Sarah gave her evidence.

Sarah had often testified in court and normally made a calm, unemotional witness. But today she was suffering from exhaustion, and the crushing weight of colossal let-down. She had the day before spent hours in Steven's company, in the witness waiting room, and he had hardly appeared to recognize her. And she had barely recognized him. How could her colleague have said he didn't look different? Or had she misremembered him? The shock, and the sinking sense that she had been building hopes on ridiculously unrealistic foundations, made her feel sick. Her determination to allocate credit where it was due was undimmed, but her capacity to do so as she had once wished, factually, unemotionally and discrediting no one except Barlow, was in shreds. As she gave her account of the attack she could hear the bitterness in her voice. She was aware of almost choking on the name 'Gitting'. The man who epitomised everything she despised in her profession. She heard herself volunteer the information that Gitting had kicked Steven's door in and entered the flat with his baton at the ready. And then, despite being offered no resistance, had handcuffed Steven in a manner she considered dangerous, given the long descent they had to make, and the young man's obvious disorientation. She sensed law-enforcement hackles in the courtroom rearing and bristling. She made an effort to moderate her tone and the next, most crucial, part of her account she gave less aggressively, though hardly with less distress. She insisted she had definitely felt herself in mortal danger from Barlow. And – although it should have been disallowed as 'opinion' – she got across the point that Steven's intervention, undertaken when handcuffed and not, at that point, in serious danger himself, was, in her view, an act of immense courage. Describing Barlow's subsequent assault on Steven she lost control and broke down, and had to take a minute to shield and dab at her eyes. During this minute nothing but ferocious scribbling from the press benches could be heard.

By the time it came to cross-examination, however, she had recovered herself. She had expressed what she wanted to in public; her mission was accomplished. She became short with her interrogator, even snappy. The defence, sensing she had lost the vulnerability she had shown earlier and wasn't going to be thrown by aggressive questioning – it might even be counter-productive – contented itself with reiterating the comparatively minor nature of her injuries.

The press were impatient to get the cross-examination over. It was obvious that Barlow was guilty, if not of attempted murder, then certainly of an offence of gross violence. They were more interested in other guilts. This young, clearly traumatised female officer had broken ranks to say things – brave things – that must have been hushed up at the time. Why? Who was responsible? And how dare they? The tabloid journalists were particularly annoyed. They thought of the opportunities they had missed. The hospital shots, in particular. The police had been deliberately withholding Steven from them. Their readers loved a hero. Who didn't?

Steven, meanwhile, in the witness waiting room throughout the afternoon, playing card games with his police minder, DC Meadows – the very officer who yesterday, if he hadn't had to nip to the Gents, would have been beside him on the court steps – heard none of Sarah's testimony. Nor did he know that his picture was in the *Independent*. He wasn't a broadsheet reader. At four o'clock he was informed that he wouldn't be called that day and, on exiting the building, found himself engulfed by a noisy sea of pressmen. Meadows hoiked him in again, but not before a dozen cameras had flashed in his face. He was so shocked he had to be propped against a corridor wall to recover. An officer went outside to issue reminders about the ban on witness interviews during court cases. The crowd insisted they just wanted photos, and to give Steven their cards. The policeman, unaware of the hostile suspicions already building, and alarmed at Steven's reaction – just what they needed, a crucial witness being panicked the day before giving evidence – told them to get stuffed. Steven was driven home via a side-door.

The next day there were more photos in the newspapers – even startled, Steven looked eye-catchingly attractive – and while, because of legal restrictions, these could be accompanied by little more than a résumé of Sarah's testimony, this was more than interesting as it stood. And today the boy himself was to give evidence. The press benches were packed.

He took the stand at eleven. Meadows, an unflappable, fatherly type, had given him a pep talk that morning, but since his panic the previous day Steven had distanced himself so far from what was about to happen that he didn't really need it. He knew what he had to say. He'd rehearsed the words over and over, like learning a script. He just had to mouth his way through them. Even if he forgot a line or two, he still had the film-memory in his head. He could always simply describe what he saw. He even remembered, as he stood facing the court, not to look at Barlow, and kept his gaze on the man who was questioning him. It was like a game really. A serious game, but nothing that touched you.

He confirmed everything Sarah had said, up to the moment Barlow had turned on him. At that point, since he had no memory of the attack, the injuries he'd sustained were listed by the prosecutor. Not listening, Steven stared down at a point on the court floor. The prosecutor then returned to the assault on Sarah and asked him directly why he had intervened to save her. Steven hesitated. He knew why the man was asking this – to add weight to the charge of attempted murder – and he knew the answer the man wanted. Which was the truth, but still seemed like something he had been told, and had had to learn. He reminded himself what it was, and then said, 'Because otherwise he was going to kill her.'

'It was clear to you, was it,' the barrister pressed, 'that the defendant was about to deliver a lethal blow to DC Grant?'

'Objection!' cried the defence.

'Yeah,' said Steven.

The barrister sat down, satisfied. The press seats purred. Coming so soon after the injury list, the corollary 'even though you must have known the risk you were taking?' hung, palpably, in the air. Then the purring turned to gasps. In the dock Barlow, furious that Steven was here at all, and now enraged beyond bearing, had leapt to his feet. Fixing Steven with slitted, malevolent eyes, he drew a pointed finger across his throat.

There was uproar. Two police officers leapt at Barlow and pushed him down. A court official rushed to the witness stand. Steven hadn't been able to stop his eyes jumping to Peter, and the flash of sensation he experienced felt like a brain seizure. After a nod from the judge he too was made to sit. The judge called an adjournment for the defendant to be removed and for the witness to be temporarily stood down. Out in the corridor Steven sat with his forearms on his thighs and his chin almost touching his knees, trying not to feel so faint. He wondered what was happening to him. Meadows was thumping his shoulder and saying, 'It's OK, Steven, you were doing great, he won't be there any more. Deep breaths, boy, deep breaths, you'll be fine.'

Fifteen minutes later Steven returned to the stand. The dock and jury benches were empty. The judge spoke kindly to him, apologized for the disruption, and told him that Barlow would not be returning. He asked if Steven felt able to continue into his cross-examination. Steven just wanted the day over, and whispered, 'Yeah.' Someone from the press benches echoed an audibly triumphant, 'Yes!'

And at that point, as it turned out, Barlow's defence collapsed. The man himself sealed this when, down in the holding cells, he first assaulted his solicitor, and then, left alone to cool down, committed criminal damage to court property. He was warned, firstly, that this case was lost and that his behaviour was just digging his grave deeper, and, secondly, that the charge of GBH to Steven could even be revised upwards in the light of events (a fanciful notion, but his solicitor was in vengeful mood). At this, in a fit of misplaced pique, Barlow sacked his lawyers and entered guilty pleas to both current charges. The jury was dismissed, the judge adjourned the court for a week for reports before sentencing, and the case was legally over.

The press were now free to write what they liked. In a three-day splurge of newsprint dozens of angles, and spin-offs from angles, were covered. Police incompetence, brutality, sexism, secrecy, and mean-mindedness. Many, without denigrating Sarah's suffering, expressed outrage at the difference in charges applied to the assaults on her and Steven. Others were fiercely critical of the fact that Barlow, with a string of violent offences behind him, should have been free at all to commit more. Never, they discovered, under the ludicrously generous remission system, had he served longer than fifteen months for any of his previous crimes. The tabloids, riding the unsung-hero line, unearthed Steven's mother. Before she realized she should be holding out for payment she was quoted as saying that Steven had always been a good boy, really, and that the shock of seeing his injuries in hospital, inflicted by her brute of an ex-husband, had been terrible. Once she clammed up a search was undertaken for Steven's natural father but, as no name was given on his birth certificate, the pursuit had to be reluctantly abandoned.

They also, of course, pursued Steven. And terrified him. He didn't know why. In the old days, when he had been confident and chaotic and carelessly criminal, he'd often dreamt of fame. Being a football star, or a racing driver. He'd once roared a stolen Jag through the estate pretending to be Damon Hill. Press attention had been part of the fame appeal. His handsome face adorning papers, magazines, the walls of teenagers' bedrooms. Who didn't have such dreams?

But now he saw his picture in the newspapers – he couldn't avoid it, cuttings were actually pushed through his letterbox – skimmed the extravagant headlines, which always included the word 'hero', and felt faint. Nauseous. He opened the door of his flat to curved lips, bared teeth and greedy faces. 'Piss off,' he told them. 'I've nothing to say.' It was as if these people were emissaries from some nightmare world, come to find him and drag him back with them. How could he speak to them? They were out to destroy him.

After the three days, frustrated with his non-cooperation and puzzled as to the reason for it – who wouldn't want to be a hero? – the press opened their ears to hints emanating from police sources. Up till now, Steven's arrest on the day of Barlow's attack – an arrest never followed with a charge – had been the sole blot on his public character. But now Steven's police record, which revealed him as a convicted drug user and thief, slid into press hands, along with alternative, speculative reasons for his 'heroism'. These were much as suggested to Sarah earlier. A few papers were reluctant to use the material – it made them look foolish, after the lavishness of their earlier praise – but many, particularly those that had held back from excess, weren't.

Steven saw only one of these articles, because he had stopped even glancing at his unsolicited mail. The day before he had torn up a letter from a model agency and a bundle of fan letters, some staggeringly lewd, sent via one of the tabloids. His next-door neighbour, a young man who was a member of a charismatic Christian group, called in to show him the offensive article and, untypically furious, told him he should sue. Steven read the article, but felt no inclination. He was upset, but only because of the unpleasant tone. The article said nothing that wasn't true. And if it meant an end to invaders on his doorstep, it could even be a blessing.

Sarah, on the other hand, saw three of the knocking reports, and was enraged. She knew immediately that police sources were responsible. The bastards. In a fever of righteous rage – amazing how energy returned with anger – she braved hostile stares at the station to call up Steven's file on the computer, which gave her his new address. And in the same visit penned a letter of resignation – an inevitability after her performance in court, and it was vital she make the first move herself – and left it on her boss's desk.

She waited impatiently till early evening, in case Steven had a job, and then drove round to his address. God, she thought, yanking on the handbrake outside his flats, I should have done this months ago. Bugger rules. She banged on his door, and, when it opened, swept inside. She had the three offensive articles in her hand. Steven hung back from her, looking alarmed.

She slapped the articles down on his living-room table and said, 'I've come to apologize for these, and to assure you that I had absolutely nothing to do with them.'

Steven stared at them. Finally he said, 'Didn't think you had. It's all right.'

'No it bloody isn't,' snapped Sarah. 'It's a disgrace.'

'Well,' said Steven. 'It's not as if . . .' He started again, diffidently. 'I mean, they're true. Kind of.'

It was Sarah's turn to stare at him. What was wrong with the man? No wonder she'd hardly recognized him at the court. Where was his spirit? His energy? He seemed so passive. So different.

'Are you all right?' she asked.

'Yeah,' he said. 'Great.'

'You don't look it.' She sniffed, staring around the room. Tidy but characterless. She couldn't associate the old Steven with a place like this. 'What are you doing with yourself these days?'

'Nothing much,' he said.

'Not working?'

'No. Still get a bit tired.' This was a lie. Exhausted, more like. Felled with fatigue. Even though there was no physical reason for it.

'So what's living in the new flat like?'

'OK.'

'Better class of neighbours, I'll bet.'

'Mmm,' said Steven.

'Made lots of new friends, have you?'

He shrugged. 'One or two. The bloke next door. Belongs to some God group. But he's OK.'

Sarah wrinkled her face up. 'A God Squadder? For Christ's sake, Steven. You be careful. Religion's catching, you know.'

Steven was shaken by her scorn. The bloke was OK. Friendly. He'd been lonely since his discharge.

'You haven't already caught it?'

'No. Course not.' He frowned. He had thought about it. Crazy, embarrassing idea. But the neighbour was nearly always happy. Happiness – that was what he would like to catch.

Sarah felt like shaking him. This wasn't the real Steven. And he must be there, underneath.

'There are other ways,' she said, suppressing the urge to bully him, and trying to sound kind. 'I know it takes a while.'

'What does?'

'Getting over things.'

He shook his head quickly. 'No no, it's not that.'

She sighed. Dear me. And she thought she'd got problems.

'Don't your old friends think you're a bit, you know, different?'

'Er . . .' He looked beyond her, vaguely. 'Don't really see old friends . . .'

'Oh Steven,' she murmured. She nearly added *what's happened to you*? But of course she knew.

He frowned and walked through to the kitchenette to plug the kettle in. Sarah was disturbing him but, at the same time, he didn't want her to go. Her manner reminded him of the hospital staff. Someone who knew it all. Like family. No threat.

Sarah saw what he was doing and said, on impulse, 'Don't do that. Have you eaten yet?'

His hand hovered over the kettle. 'No. Why?'

She stood up. This flat was depressing. And a cup of tea at seven pm, as if they were pensioners . . . 'Grab a jacket,' she said. 'You need to get out more. My treat.'

He didn't object. She wondered if he objected to anything these days. She drove him to a restaurant in the centre of the city. An Italian restaurant. It just happened to be her favourite. Steven had never been to a proper restaurant before – one that opened at six and closed at midnight, and didn't serve take-away curry and chips – but didn't mention this. As they sat down at their table the newness of the experience caused him to say, out of awkwardness more than anything else, 'My dad was Italian.'

'Was he?' said Sarah, interested. 'Really? Where is he now?'

'Italy, I suppose. Dunno. Never knew him. Mum says he was only here for a weekend.'

'Christ,' sighed Sarah. 'Well, Italy's wonderful. You should go there. See for yourself.'

'Mmm,' said Steven.

'And,' said Sarah, picking up the printed list in front of them, 'their wine is fantastic. The red, anyway. I'll get us a bottle.'

She enjoyed watching him eat the food she recommended and kept his wine glass topped up. Since she had the car she limited herself to one glass. She told him she'd resigned from the police force though she didn't explain why; just said she'd had enough. He didn't seem surprised, or even interested. After they'd finished the main course and were waiting for the menu again, she studied him, decided he looked mellow and relaxed, and said, 'I've wanted to see you for months, Steven.'

'Have you?' He gave her a small smile. The first she'd seen. Not a smile, though, like his old smiles. 'Why?'

'I'd have thought that was obvious. To thank you for

what you did. To see how you were. To talk about what happened.'

His smile faded. He looked away.

'It is important, you know,' she stressed. 'I mean, it was a big thing. And there was just you and me—'

He was shaking his head, frowning. 'I don't remember much.'

'Oh come on. You gave evidence.'

'Well, yeah.' He shifted in his seat. 'Thing is, I don't really like talking about it.'

'I know.' She smiled understandingly. 'Tedious, isn't it, saying it over and over.' She caught herself. Why she had uttered such an idiocy? Such a blatant untruth. Who had she talked it 'over and over' with? Properly. Only her counsellor. She had been waiting for Steven.

She had just opened her mouth, a retraction on the tip of her tongue, when a red-faced man pushed past to lean over the table. He was wearing a coat beaded with raindrops, as if he'd just walked in off the street. He peered into Steven's face, then smiled triumphantly and said, 'Steven? It is, isn't it? I'm from the *Evening News*. You'll excuse me interrupting—'

'No,' Sarah cut in, outraged. 'He won't. This is a private conversation. Sod off.'

'Charming,' said the man. 'And you are? Oh my my, DC Grant.'

Steven had pushed his chair back. He looked wild-eyed, as if he was about to bolt.

'Waiter!' Sarah called quickly. She waved one of the dark-suited Italians over. 'This man is bothering us. Please remove him.'

'OK, OK.' The newsman raised his palms, backing off.

Sarah held Steven's eyes across the table, reassuring him. She waited until the man had been escorted from the premises and then said, 'Relax. There's nothing wrong with what we're doing. I promise. Even if I had still been a policewoman.'

'S'not that.'

'What is it then?'

'Those people. Knocking at my door.'

'I know. Monstrous.' She caught herself again. Monstrous? Annoying, maybe. But he'd actually looked frightened . . .

'Steven,' she said, puzzling. 'Do you ever have dreams? About what happened?'

'No.' He shook his head definitely.

'Flashbacks? When a scene comes back to you—?'

'No. No. Nothing.'

'What, so you don't think about it at all?'

'No. Unless—' He cast a dark look at the door. 'Why should I? It's over.'

'Well,' said Sarah. 'It's about sorting things out in your head. So you can move on.'

'Don't need to,' said Steven. 'I have moved on. Everything's different.'

'Yes,' said Sarah gently. 'I can see that.'

He stared at her. His eyes appeared moist, or maybe it was just the light.

'Look at yourself, Steven,' she murmured.

He continued to stare at her, and then dropped his gaze and mumbled, 'Think I want to go back soon.'

'OK,' she sighed.

After she dropped him off she went home herself and curled up in an armchair. It was sad. Steven had saved her life, but somehow lost his own. He didn't seem to understand what had happened to him. She sighed over this a while and then, as if the thought had plugged itself into her mental processes, and was now flashing lights at her, realised it might be literally true. That his knowledge was actually deficient. Christ. Of course it would be. He didn't remember the attack on himself. So the last thing he'd be able to recall would be . . . slinging the crowbar? Barlow roaring at him? And then: nothing, till he came round in hospital. That had happened gradually. And he'd been sedated. Days and days missing. Who would have filled in the gap for him? Who could have? Who knew, except herself? The police wouldn't have shown him her statement. Or quoted from it. Of course not. And later? Now? He hadn't been in court when she testified. It wasn't allowed. And she bet he hadn't read the newspaper accounts. Anyway, they were partial versions. Opinionated versions. They didn't tell the truth.

But, of course, he didn't want to know. Now. And he couldn't be forced.

Maybe, though, she thought, he could learn from example. It was nearly midnight but she felt suddenly wide awake. Urgent. He had saved her life. She'd do it now. She picked up a pen and on a sheet of writing paper wrote: *Read this, Steven, please. Don't worry, it's not about you. It's about me.*

Then on the next few pages, she wrote down exactly what had happened that morning at the block of flats, entirely from her perspective. Not just the events, as she remembered them, but what she had felt. Even thoughts and feelings she would have been mortified to admit to face to face. Such as how attractive he had looked to her when she and Gitting had woken him. How terrified she had been when she was flung into the empty flat. As if Barlow had stripped her of her clothes, not just the radio. And how dreadful the sight of Barlow attacking him had been. How the kicking had gone on and on, viciously, obscenely pointless, and how appalled and guilty she had felt. How the picture had returned to her in nightmares, again and again.

Then she wrote about her feelings afterwards. How relieved
she had been to see him alive, in Intensive Care. How upset
when her superiors refused to publicly acknowledge his
bravery. God, she thought, looking up from the paper. If
they'd done as she'd asked, Steven would have been
forced to talk about it, the moment he was capable. He'd
have been forced to grasp what had happened. Everyone
would have been interested. And that would have been
the right time. Bloody, bastard colleagues. She put her
head down again and wrote about her distress in the
following months, her flashbacks and nightmares, how
difficult she had found work, and how she had longed to
see him, to express her gratitude and to talk about it, but
had had to make do with pouring it out to a counsellor.
And he had had no one. She didn't write this. She was
sticking to her word. But he'd hadn't. She was sure he
hadn't. Poor Steven. He hadn't returned to his old flat, his
old mates, his old life. No reminders. Never had to explain
anything to anyone. Not even to himself. No wonder. No
wonder.

When she'd finished she didn't bother to read it through.
She'd only end up getting cold feet about sending it. She
wrote her address on the top, stuffed the sheets into an
envelope, and ran out to the post box at the end of the
road. That's it, she said to herself, as she released it through
the slot. I don't suppose I'll ever see him again, but I've
done my best. Then she went home, and in bed at last – it
was now 4.00am – sank deep into the bedding. Her neck
muscles were so relaxed she knew she'd be asleep in
seconds. Her last thought was that writing the letter might
have done her good, too.

When Steven received the handwritten envelope, a day
and a few hours later, he nearly tore it up without opening
it. Most similar letters, on other days, had met this fate. But

the thickness and weight of the envelope stopped him. It felt as if it contained something besides paper, and by the time he'd discovered it didn't he had read the lines on the first page of the bundle, and automatically flicked to the end to see who it was from. Sarah. He put the bundle down instantly, as if it were toxic. But he didn't throw it away. Just left it on the table.

He busied himself with small activities in the flat for several hours, wishing he had something to do that would make him, truly, forget about the pages on the table. But he had nothing to occupy him outside the flat, and little within. What did he do with his time, usually? It was as if he was so internally occupied – with what? with what? – that there was no space left over for the outside world.

He picked up the pages again at four in the afternoon. He'd have to read them sometime. He read them standing by the living-room table. He didn't know how long it took. Ages. An eon of words. An eon of squiggles on a page. When he'd finished he put the pages down. Then found himself in the kitchenette without knowing how he'd got there. He made himself a mug of tea, then abandoned it to return to the sitting room and reread the pages. This time they made more sense. He understood them. But so what? So what? He knew most of it already.

He switched on the television and sat down. A year ago he hardly ever watched TV – on the rare occasions he was in, he listened to music. One of the few virtues of those old flats was that no one complained about loud music. But, anyway, television rooted you more, filled more of your senses.

At nine in the evening he acknowledged that he was restless. That he had been ignoring – even fighting – an impulse to move his limbs. To do something, go somewhere. But what, where?

He put his jacket on and left the flat. He heard himself make a noise in his throat as he banged the foyer door shut behind him. He was annoyed that Sarah had sent him that letter. This was her fault. He was choked up with annoyance. He needed to walk the feeling off.

He strode in the direction of the local shops and pub, but then, making another involuntary, frustrated noise, swung round and strode in the opposite direction. He'd get it all over with, in one evening. Otherwise this might go on for days. Fuck Sarah.

It took him an hour and a half to walk back to his old block of flats. Jeez, they looked depressing. Even in the dark. Especially in the dark. There were small mountains of cardboard rubbish either side of the block entrance. Broken glass crunched underfoot. What a dump this place was. Literally. He hated it. He certainly had no regrets. He was glad he'd moved.

He thought he might go up to his old flat. Just go up in the lifts, look out at the city from the walkway outside his old front door – not a bad view, at night – and walk down again. That should do it. Get it out of his system.

The lifts were working. The one he used smelt, though. Piss: could be animal or human. He vaguely remembered pissing in one of the lifts himself once. Too drunk to contemplate the stairs, and then, waiting for it to crank its slow way up, just doing it. The place was so crap it deserved to be pissed on.

He stepped out on to the eighth floor. Behind him the closing doors squealed in their runners and slapped shut, cutting off the bright light. But the caged-in emergency bulb above was working. He could still see. He stepped into his old walkway.

The council had mended his front door. Or replaced it. But the kitchen window beyond was boarded up. No one wanted his old flat, presumably. Well, he certainly didn't. He turned to lean on the chest-high railings of the walkway, and stared down.

Nothing moved in the gloom below. He could hear the distant whooping shouts of teenage boys. The staccato bark of a disturbed dog. And another. Then an even more faraway shout. Female. The background rumble of traffic. Normal, night sounds. He lifted his gaze to the orange glow of the city beyond.

It came to him that nothing meant much to him any more. If he did feel anything, it was always negative. Something he didn't want to feel.

And he didn't belong anywhere. Not here, any more, and not in his new flat. He hadn't made it into a home. Other tenants managed to stamp character on their flats, but he hadn't. He couldn't do it. It was just a space.

Perhaps the answer was that he had no character. That he was no character. That he didn't really exist. Perhaps Peter had actually killed him, in that flat two floors below, and everything that had happened since was a kind of dying dream. Looking back, it felt dreamlike. Would he feel like this forever? Or just till something else happened?

If something else was going to happen, he wished it would happen quickly.

He pulled himself away from the rails and walked to the top of the stairs. He looked down. They were just stairs.

He blanked his mind, and set off down. Fast. He could hear nothing, absolutely nothing, except the sound of his own feet clattering on concrete. He supposed it must be eleven or so. The block could be empty, dead. Seventh floor. Sixth floor. Made it past that, anyway. Fifth floor. They were all the same.

He stopped suddenly at the half landing below the fifth floor. Shit. The light wasn't working below. His heart raced.

Who'd have thought that running down stairs could make you so breathless? He crept down a couple more steps, peering over the handrail, hoping to see a glimmer of light shining up from the third floor. Nothing. He gripped the metal. Well, all he had to do was hang on to this. It would guide him down.

But he couldn't do it. His legs wouldn't move. The blackness below was too black. Too dangerous. Too fearsome. It could be concealing anything. He couldn't descend into blackness like that.

He'd have to go back up to the lift. Go down the easy, mechanical way, the nearest doors just a short stair-flight away. He would shut himself in the bright, piss-scented metal box and by-pass the blackness. Forget about it. There was no one here to witness his retreat, no one would know.

But to move upwards he would have to release his grip on the handrail, and, he discovered, he couldn't do that, either. It was all that was stopping him from falling forward into the blackness. As he thought this an excruciating sensation passed through him. A wave of vertiginous terror, curling his toes, making him sway with dizziness. He was going to fall. No, he mustn't. He gripped the handrail tighter and lowered himself, carefully, inch by inch, to the concrete. Felt at last the cold solidity of a concrete step under his backside. The terror subsided to pounding, containable fear. He was safe. Safe, but stuck. Like a climber paralysed on a cliff face.

Sarah was right, he thought dimly. 'Look at yourself,' she'd said. Such pity in her face. Well, yes, look at him. Pathetic. Something was terribly wrong with him.

But what could he do about it? Nothing. The damage, whatever it was, had been done. The only answer was not to have been who he had been, not to have become what he had become. To start again, right from the beginning. Which was impossible.

He wondered how long he would have to sit here before someone found him. If anyone did come, would they come up from the darkness, or down from the light? Would they help him? Or hurt him? Or just stare at him, as they passed by? See him as someone helpless, disintegrating. Unhelpable. This last thought was so distressing it tugged at his mouth. He had to close his eyes and pushed his face into his sleeve.

The only answer left, then, was to erase everything.

No one came. He remained sitting on the step, tethered by his hand to the grab rail, until it grew light. Hours and hours. He heard lifts hiss and clank up and down several times, and a few doors bang. But saw no one on the stairs. The cold seeped into him, upwards from his buttocks, downwards from his bare hand on the metal. His fingers seemed to have frozen on to the rail. Maybe he dozed a bit. Whether he did or not, the light seemed to come suddenly. Suddenly it was just concrete steps below. Nothing to be frightened of. Empty concrete.

He tried to get up. Failed the first time, made it the second. Unclamped his stiff fingers from the rail. Very cautiously, jerkily, he descended the stairs. He had a pain in his head, above his eyes, like the pain from eating ice-cream straight from a freezer.

He didn't think he could walk all the way home. Not this cold and stiff. There was a mini-cab office round the corner. He didn't know how early it opened, but it had a recessed, sheltered entrance, and he shouldn't have to wait long. He had money in his pocket.

The owner turned up within fifteen minutes. Masud. He even recognized Steven. Said in his fruity, friendly voice, 'Gracious, Steven boy, what an early bird!' as if he'd never noticed he'd been away. He let Steven wait in the office until the first driver arrived. By seven Steven was in the passenger seat of a warm Granada, being sped through the city streets.

He got himself dropped off at his local shops. One of the conveniences of the new flat was that it was only a two-minute walk from a small parade, with a mini-mart, a launderette and a chemist. The chemist wasn't open yet but the mini-mart was. He went to the checkout counter, where tobacco and medicines were sold, and asked for aspirin. What sized pack? the man asked. Oh, largest you got, said Steven. The man handed him a paper bag and charged him thirty pence. Outside on the pavement Steven opened the bag and saw that the pack inside contained only sixteen tablets. Shit, he thought. Shit. He went back into the shop and said actually he'd been after a bottle. Fifty, or a hundred. The man said they didn't exist any longer. Not for aspirin or paracetamol, because people kept using them to top themselves. Can I have another pack, then, Steven asked, flustered, and the man shrugged and said sure.

He walked home quickly. He was tired. Dead-beat tired. Still had a thumping headache. He was longing to go to bed. Was thirty-two enough? Yeah, must be. Sixteen times a normal dose. Must be.

He couldn't remember when he'd last taken aspirin. In the hospital they always gave you paracetamol. He hated the taste of paracetamol. Unless you washed them cleanly down with the first gulp of water, they made you want to gag. But aspirins, he seemed to remember, weren't too bad.

He made himself a large pot of weak tea and drank two mugs of it, with lots of sugar, and swallowed sixteen aspirin tablets per mug. No problem. He was so tired he could see his eyelashes fluttering. He went through to the bedroom, stripped down to his boxer shorts, and fell into bed. He was asleep in seconds.

Six hours later, at two in the afternoon, Sarah received a visitor. DC Meadows. She knew him vaguely, and didn't hate him. He was OK. Steven's minder.

'Not going to beat around the bush,' he said abruptly. 'Is Steven here?'

She goggled at him. 'No.'

'It's not a problem if he is.' He sighed suddenly. 'Just need to find him.'

'Well he's not,' Sarah said. 'What on earth made you think he would be?'

'Um. Just a rumour . . .'

God, Sarah groaned inwardly. The sniggering grapevine. 'Why d'you want him?'

'He's asked to be in court day after tomorrow. For after the sentencing. Judge wants to say a few words.'

'Does he now.' Sarah considered this. It could only mean that the judge was going to commend him in some way. 'Good, good.'

'But I can't find him,' said Meadows. 'He wasn't at his flat nine thirty last night, nor at eleven, nor at ten this morning. D'you know where he hangs out?'

'Mmm. Not sure he does much hanging out these days. He really wasn't there this morning?' To herself, she thought: he would have got my letter yesterday . . .

'Well,' said Meadows cautiously. 'He wasn't answering, anyway. I banged on the door for quite a while. You have seen him recently, haven't you? Is he all right? I mean, would you say—'

'No,' said Sarah, knowing exactly what he was about to ask. 'Or yes, rather. He could be upset.' Oh God, she prayed, please don't let me have hurt him again. Please God. She grabbed a coat from the hall rack. 'I'm coming with you.'

Steven lay in bed, blinking up at the ceiling. He was achingly hungry. And yet he should be dead. He had already seen on the CD player across the room that it was past two in the afternoon. He had gone to bed before eight this morning. Six hours ago. After taking thirty two aspirin. So why was he awake? Alive. Why hadn't the aspirin worked?

He sat up. Nothing unpleasant kicked in with the change of position. In fact he felt fine. His headache had gone completely. Thirty-two aspirin, and all that had happened was his headache was cured.

He swung his legs over the side of the bed, and found the tablets. The oddest sight. They were lying in a rough circle on the carpet, about an arm's length across. Densely packed in the centre, thinly scattered at the outside. As if they had been fired from an aspirin gun. A few, he noticed, hadn't even made it to the carpet, and were stuck to the side of the mattress. And, now he looked closely, he could see a slight darkening of the mauve-grey carpet around them. A sort of damp ring. And there was a faint acrid smell.

Why was there nothing except aspirin? When had he last eaten? Had he eaten *anything*, since receiving Sarah's letter? Shit. His stomach must have been completely empty.

He counted the aspirin. They'd hardly decomposed at all. He could still see the indent on most where they could be split in half. His body must have revolted almost immediately. Some were stuck together. He counted twenty-six on the floor, five glued to the side of the bed.

He didn't remember vomiting. But he must have. Just thrown the lot up, soon after he fell asleep. Aspirin and tea and nothing else.

He didn't know what he felt about this. About being still alive. Weird. Hard to get his head round. And he was not only alive, but thoroughly, healthily alive. As if he hadn't contemplated being not alive at all.

His stomach felt concave. He dressed quickly. If these tablets had lain here for six hours they could lie a bit longer while he ate something. In the kitchenette he put eight slices of bread on the cooker grill and got out the margarine, jam, and peanut butter. He threw the empty aspirin packets into the swing bin.

He was on his fourth slice of toast when someone banged on the door. Instantly it came to him that someone had banged earlier. A banging he'd half heard, and ignored.

A male voice called, 'Steven!' Then another voice, female, cried, 'Steven!' Both sounded urgent. Still holding the toast, he stepped through to the tiny hallway and opened the door. Meadows and Sarah.

'What's wrong?' Their faces told him something was. Though their expressions were loosening now. Relaxing to smiles.

'Nothing,' said Sarah. 'Having an unnecessary panic. Phew.' She jerked her head at Meadows. 'He's been trying to get hold of you. Last night and this morning. You got us a bit worried.'

'Oh, right,' said Steven. 'Well, you've found me now.'

'Yes.' Sarah looked ridiculously pleased.

'Got a message for you,' Meadows said. 'You're wanted in court. Judge's request. Day after tomorrow.'

Steven groaned. 'Do I have to?'

Sarah eyed Meadows hard and said, 'Yes, you do.'

'You won't have to say anything,' Meadows assured him. 'As long as the judge can see you. No witness stands. No big deal. Promise. Tell you what, I'll take you. Same as before. Just be here, nine o'clock. Right?'

He waited till Steven nodded reluctant agreement, then stepped away from the door. Sarah dithered and said, 'Ah, just want to have a word with Steven. Don't worry about me, I'll find my own way back.'

'Fine,' said Meadows, neutrally.

They watched him leave.

'You going to invite me in, then?' Sarah asked.

'Sure,' said Steven. Sarah was always very bossy and familiar with him, he thought. He supposed he didn't mind.

He walked through to the kitchenette to get his fifth slice of toast, while Sarah threw her coat over the back of one of the sitting room chairs. She could see her letter to him on the table. Pages and pages of it.

She nodded at it as he wandered back. 'You read it then.'

'Yeah,' said Steven.

'Did you find it interesting?'

He shrugged. Didn't know what to say. Interesting? Yeah, so interesting I stayed out all night, terrified and nearly freezing to death on a concrete stairway, and then took thirty-two aspirins. He remembered he'd been angry with her yesterday for sending it. Couldn't work up much anger about it now, though.

'When Meadows said he couldn't raise you I got this terrible feeling that I might have upset you. That you'd read the letter and got upset, and . . . you know . . . Sorry. I know it's stupid.'

'I'm fine,' said Steven. He bit into the toast and peanut butter.

'Yes. On the way over, I was thinking, first I nearly get you killed by Barlow, and then I finish you off myself, telling you about it.' She laughed gaily. 'I'm amazingly relieved. You can probably tell.'

Steven stopped chewing. Astonishing. It hadn't crossed his mind that taking the aspirins would have had an effect on anyone except himself. Sarah would have minded. She wasn't acting. He believed her.

And, of course, as it had turned out, taking the aspirins hadn't even affected himself. That was kind of funny, he now saw.

'You don't have to worry about going to court,' Sarah was saying. 'It can only be because the judge wants to thank you.'

'Really? Shit. Will I have to see Peter?'

'Don't see why. Tell them you don't want to. He'll get life, you know. Attempted murder's the same as murder. Might get life for the GBH too. It's possible. You can forget about him.'

It occurred to Steven that Sarah was full of contradictions. Telling him to forget about Peter, just after sending a letter forcing reminders on him. He could see the man himself, today, very clearly. As if he had just stepped out of the dark. Real for the first time . . . well, he wanted to say, *in his life*; but he must have been real before. In *this* life. That was nearer. Peter. His mother's husband. His stepfather, though he'd never thought of him as that, and Peter had certainly never acted like a father. A bastard, more like. The bastard who had caused all this trouble, and who he had just helped send to gaol. He could hardly believe this. He was helping the police to lock Peter up! But shit, why not, after what he'd done? The maniac had nearly killed him. He deserved it. And he didn't remember feeling too scared while he was doing it. Just that one freak-out moment. In fact the prospect of going to court day after tomorrow felt more daunting.

'Will you be there?' he asked.

'Try and stop me,' said Sarah.

The courtroom wasn't as packed as it had been the day Steven testified, but it was noisier. Steven, slipping into the courtroom behind Meadows during a five minute recess, noticed neither the crowd present, nor the end-of-term buzz in the air. Just his own intense rawness. He concentrated on following Meadows' suited back, and found himself in a seat in the well of the court. He could have reached out and touched the stiff collar of one the prosecution clerks. He knew already, because someone had just told them, that Peter had got life, twice, with a minimum term of twelve years. Just words. Sarah was here somewhere, Meadows said he'd seen her.

The room rose as the judge entered. The murmur in the courtroom died. The judge mounted his podium and peered down at Steven and Meadows over the gold rims of his half-moon glasses. His lips pressed together in satisfaction. He sat down and spread his arms across the wood to either side of him in a godlike, final-arbiter stance. Everyone else sat down. Steven dropped his eyes and studied his knees.

The judge had a loud theatrical voice, and an indirect way of speaking. Perhaps this was just an introduction. He was talking about end-notes, setting records straight, and drawing firm lines somewhere or other.

The voice paused for a moment. Bottoms shifted. Steven glanced quickly over his shoulder. Sarah was right at the back. He couldn't catch her eye though; she was staring past him, towards the judge.

Who was speaking again. Steven felt his arm nudged by Meadows. The judge was talking about a witness whose testimony had been crucially important to the case. Without whom the defendant, almost certainly, could not have been convicted. Although it seemed unlikely, Steven guessed this witness was himself. The young man who had given this testimony, the judge said, was, as it happened, also the prime victim, who had suffered most at the hands of the accused, and who had most cause, for this and other historical and domestic reasons, to fear him. Steven picked at a loose thread in the seam of his trousers. This felt like personal stuff. Uncomfortable.

To confront those fears and speak out, the judge said (his voice actually lifted and swelled as he said it) had taken great courage.

No it hadn't. This was embarrassing.

But perhaps if he substituted the fears he had felt at his old flat, that night he couldn't move? Well, no, because he hadn't had much choice about confronting them. Hadn't known they were going to leap out at him. And anyway, he hadn't faced them with anything that felt like courage. It had felt like terror.

Almost as much courage, the judge was continuing, as this same witness had shown eight months ago, when he had saved the life of a young policewoman.

This was excruciating. He hadn't made a decision to do that. Just . . . what? Reflex?

Funnily enough, the words sailing over him were about this. Or perhaps he'd been listening without realizing it. Altruism, the judge was talking about. Steven risked a quick glance upwards. It was safe. The judge was eyeing not him, but the press benches behind him. Severely. He was telling them that 'the altruism of this witness's actions was not to be questioned'. Certain unpleasantnesses, apparently, had been brought to his attention this week, which had now to stop. He sounded fierce. Everyone, he went on, had heard the testimony of DC Sarah Grant, who was the only person in any position to make a valid judgement in this matter, and she had made her opinion perfectly clear. The court trusted DC Grant, because she had been there, and because she had no reason to distort the truth. Others should likewise trust her. They should also understand that altruistic actions were not less altruistic because they had been performed instinctively. This merely indicated a deeply ingrained regard for what was right. A natural goodness.

Steven's throat had started to ache. For a horrible moment he thought he was going to cry. And yet he didn't feel sad. Just unprotected. Skinned.

In recognition of all he had just said, the judge went on, and to underline the court's gratitude to this particular witness, he intended to make him a small discretionary award. A mere token, in financial terms, since the court's funds were extremely limited, but one which was intended to express a very large measure of goodwill. He had combined this token award with a sum offered freely by the city's police force, who wished also to acknowledge and reward the conduct of this witness.

A small outbreak of coughing from the back of the room interrupted him. The judge waited till it subsided and then said, firmly, that such an expression of gratitude at the conclusion of the case had always been the Chief Constable's intention. He paused, as if challenging throats to choke again. None did.

The total amounted to six hundred pounds. He smiled warmly down at Steven and said that if the witness would allow the liberty of a recommendation, he would suggest that this sum be used for a treat. Perhaps to take himself off on holiday, somewhere he could relax and start to put behind him the ordeal he had been through.

Sarah rushed up to Steven and Meadows in the corridor outside the courtroom. 'Right, you know where to go. Got a passport?'

'Err . . .' Steven was feeling overwhelmed. He couldn't seem to switch off like he used to. He needed time to calm himself.

'You've got to go to Italy,' Sarah said impatiently. 'Obviously.'

'Eh?' said Meadows.

Sarah didn't bother to explain. She pushed her arm through Steven's and led him out of the court house. 'Sod off,' she said to any member of the press who approached them. Though Steven didn't seem nearly so alarmed by them now.

'OK.' Sarah slapped the passport forms they'd just picked up from the post office on to the pub table in front of them. 'The judge is right. You need to treat yourself. Reward yourself. It's important.'

Steven frowned down at the forms. He felt as if he was holding his breath. Only trivia was safe. Information booklets, special envelopes . . .

Meadows distributed drinks and, over Steven's head, said to Sarah, 'Has he got someone he could go with? A bit lonely, holidaying on your own . . .'

'Don't look at me,' said Sarah. 'Hardly going to forget with me around, is he? Anyway, you meet more people on your own.' She nudged Steven's elbow. 'Oi. Leave those. Listen. Be brave. Get an open return ticket, coach, plane, whatever, and stay till your money runs out. Should give you a good two or three weeks, this time of year.'

'This is a hell of a form, ' Steven said, faintly.

'Oh for God's sake,' groaned Sarah. 'Don't be so negative. I'll sort out your passport for you. If that's all that's stopping you.'

Is it? Steven thought. No. He wasn't being negative. Just tiptoeing onto unbelievable luck. Testing its strength. But Sarah thought it could happen. She sounded so sure. And he did trust her. What was it he'd said to himself, that night at the old flats? As an alternative to erasing everything? Start all over again. Right from the beginning. Which was impossible, of course. Had been, and still was. But going to Italy. It was where part of him had started . . .

'I don't speak Italian,' he murmured. Let Sarah cut the last lifeline.

'Oh shut up,' she said. 'Who does? If you don't go I shall turn up at your flat every evening and sneer at you. Tell you how pathetic you are—'

'Looks like you got no choice, boy,' said Meadows.

Afterwards, simply for her own sake, Sarah wished she hadn't pushed him so effectively. That he hadn't gone quite so quickly. And, given her time again, she'd have made a bigger deal of saying goodbye to him at Gatwick Airport. Something more than, 'You'll be OK now, won't you?' out of the car window at the drop-off spot, because she couldn't be bothered to find somewhere to park. But, of course, she didn't know his intentions.

'Send me a postcard!' she'd shouted after him. But a fortnight passed, then a month, and none came. She was applying to train as a probation officer and in the meantime was working as a store detective in her local M&S. Three months on she was driving past Steven's flat on her way to a date with the M&S Food Hall manager, who was thirty and single and someone she might, possibly, be falling in love with. She had allowed far too much time and didn't want to embarrass herself by arriving early. So she stopped off at Steven's flat and banged on the door. A young couple were living there. Had been for three weeks. They didn't know the previous tenant, sorry.

Weird, she thought. Where is he?

A letter arrived in late September. She'd moved herself by then, into a flat she and the Food Hall manager were renting jointly. He wouldn't let her cook. He was bliss. She tore the envelope open, seeing the Italian stamps above the forwarded-on address label, but found nothing inside except a folded piece of blank paper protecting a photo. She studied it. It was a group shot of seven people, lined up in bright sunlight against a pink-flowering hedge. She didn't recognize anyone. But this had to be from Steven; he must be the photographer. In the centre were a middle-aged couple, both darkly handsome and beautifully dressed. Very stylish. Very Italian. Either side of them were three young women, girls really, two one side, one the other. All three with brown hair, olive-shaped eyes and innocently toothy smiles. Then flanking these five, one each end of the line, two young men. Very handsome young men, dark and smiling. Not with innocent toothiness though. With confidence, even arrogance. Hmm. Very Italian, too. The younger generation were wearing some sort of livery. Green jackets with a gold motif on the breast pocket. A family business? That's what it looked like. Or were there too many of them? Perhaps five young employees, and their parental employers? No way of knowing. And the nature of the business? Again, obscure. Sarah turned the photo over. Ah, names. A list, in block capitals. 'Franco – Vittoria – Carla – Signora Ginoli – Giovanni Ginoli – Sophia'. Steven must work with these people. Great, great. Below the names were three words in Italian. *Ciao bella, Stefano*. Stefano? Of course, Steven. She grinned. Then looked at the list of names again. Funny. Why only six? She flipped the photo over. Good God. The young man on the right. Next to Sophia. Was that Steven? Stefano? It was! She laughed out loud. Jesus, look at that smile! How *disgraceful*. What a smoothie! 'Ciao bella', indeed. Cheeky sod.

She grinned at the photo for a while. It was making a mush of her insides. Oh Steven, she told it, I don't know what you've sorted for yourself, but this looks OK. It really does. You look a new person. Hi beautiful yourself, Steven.